# Why have you never married ?

a novel by
F. M. Cipriano

FMC Press

# Why have you never married ?

[ ISBN 978-0-9941743-5-2 ]
First published 2019 by FMC Press
PO Box 13179
Law Courts VIC 8010
Australia
Copyright © F. M. Cipriano 2019
Book Cover: Rachmad Ridwan
Editing & Proofreading: Nicola Markus

 A catalogue record for this
book is available from the
National Library of Australia

Published by FMC Press

www.fmcpress.com

# Acknowledgements

This book was inspired by my early life experiences and I acknowledge the people who were closest to me and who provided me with tremendous support.

My eternal gratitude goes to my dearly departed parents, Porzia and Giuseppe Cipriano, whose nurturing, dedication and love will always stay in my heart and my memories.

I fondly look back to my early years when I grew up in a loving, close-knit family, being the youngest of three children with my dear sisters, Maria Prolisko and Clara O'Bryan.

I greatly appreciate the favour granted to me by Harry Christopher, an enduring friend, who reviewed those parts of the book concerning the Audit Office.

I also extend my gratitude to Michael Schembri, a good friend, who read this book, as well as every one of my four previous books, and provided me with useful feedback every time.

# About the Author

F. M. Cipriano (Frank) was born in Melbourne, Australia. He has a Bachelor of Business, a Graduate Diploma in Accounting, a Diploma of Financial Services, and a Master of Taxation.

Frank was a career public servant with the Australian Taxation Office (ATO) until he gained a voluntary redundancy, departing on 29 August 2014.

Since leaving the ATO, Frank has pursued his passion for writing. His previously published books are:

*A Bachelor's Travels* – March 2015
*My Taxing Career* – March 2017
*A Working Holiday* – February 2018
*White Man Dreaming* – February 2018

Frank's latest novel is inspired by his early years, from his happy family upbringing, to his disciplined Catholic education, and the harsh realities of young adult life.

# Table of Contents

# Chapter 1

## It's a Date

After having completed the three S's — shit, shower, and shave — I stood fully nude in front of my full-length bedroom mirror, focussing on my lifetime battle scars, and reflecting on what could have been if things had turned out differently. *What if I had been born an average-looking person and lived a normal life?*

Snapping out of my momentary daze, I shuffled over to my bedroom cupboard and swung the double doors wide open. I inspected my clothes with serious intent, mixing and matching a number of combinations before I settled on one of my standard get-ups — black jeans, white shirt, and dark-blue blazer.

It was a highly conventional ensemble, but I was never one to want to stand out in a crowd.

The overnight weather forecast was for 10 degrees centigrade with occasional showers. Stepping out in the early evening, I felt a chill as the cool air gusted through.

I hopped into my 1988 red MG Convertible, which I had purchased new 10 years ago. It only had

50,000 kilometres on the clock and I kept it immaculate.

When I backed out of the garage and onto the road, a light shower sprinkled over the windscreen, and I flicked on the intermittent windscreen wipers.

As I drove across the city of Melbourne, from the northern inner suburb of Carlton to the eastern suburb of Camberwell, I was pensive about my date.

I had met Dorothy through an internet dating site, which assessed us to be a 'perfect match'.

Dorothy was a 33-year-old teacher who'd had a series of long-term relationships, although she had never been married and had no children.

Our first date resulted out of a culmination of a few emails, an initial meeting, and a number of subsequent telephone conversations spanning over the week.

We got on famously when we first met for coffee and our subsequent conversations had been engaging and entertaining, so I was optimistic that the evening would be enjoyable.

I pulled up outside Dorothy's house and made my way to the front gate, which squeaked as I swung it open. I strode towards the house with my black leather boots making loud clicking sounds as they echoed off the concrete path.

I rang the doorbell and my mind wandered as I anticipated a response. I was a little nervous, but not as nervous as I thought I should have been. After all, I was 40 and it was my first ever formal date.

The front door eventually creaked open and Dorothy greeted me wearing a tight-fitting black velvet dress hemmed just above the knee. Contrasting her dark dress was the bright glow of the porch light reflecting off her bleached-blonde hair, deep blue eyes, and dazzling single-string pearl necklace.

"You look radiant," I commented.

"Let's not overdo it," she replied.

"No, I mean it. You're giving off so much of a glow that I could do with a pair of sunglasses."

We both laughed.

I escorted her to my car and guided her into the front passenger seat before I got in and drove to a fancy teppanyaki restaurant. We enjoyed a lively discussion over some hot and cold sake before being entertained by the chef who masterly grilled various foods on the iron plate as he juggled his kitchen utensils and cracked jokes.

"Catch this with your mouth," the chef instructed as he pointed to Dorothy and flipped a small piece of prawn in her direction, which she snapped up to the cheers and applause of the other diners.

The chef repeated the exercise with her a couple more times before he indicated it was my turn.

"No, no, no," I pleaded, but I saw a piece of prawn hurtling towards me.

I tried to rise to catch the food in my mouth, but it hit me square on my upper lip to the laughs and jeers of the other diners.

"Okay, that's enough," I said, but another morsel

was soon on its way.

I opened my mouth wide as I swayed to catch the piece of prawn, but it reflected off my cheek, again to the jeers and even louder laughs of the other diners.

I was convinced the prick of a chef was making wayward throws on purpose. "Okay, that is definitely enough," I stated.

"No, you have to get at least one," Dorothy insisted.

The chef then started flipping a series of pieces of food towards me. I was infuriated when the first one hit me on the lapel of my blazer. The second was heading for my chest, but I caught it in my hands and popped it into my mouth. A third headed for my face while I was munching on the previous prawn, so I also caught that one in my hands. It wasn't until I gestured that I was about to throw the food back at the chef that he finally stopped tossing things at me.

The chef proceeded on to the other diners with mixed success.

I was relieved when we could enjoy the remainder of the dinner in a more civilised manner — using chopsticks.

"You don't seem to have very good co-ordination like I do," Dorothy said with a smile.

I also smiled as I replied. "Maybe you could easily catch the food because you've got such a big mouth."

We both laughed.

I drove Dorothy home and turned off the engine.

"Thanks for the lovely evening," she said.

"It was my pleasure."

"I'll give you a call."

"Okay. Goodnight."

Dorothy allowed me to give her a peck on the lips before I headed home.

# Chapter 2

## Post-Date

I was surprised when Dorothy rang me during the following week, and we agreed to a rendezvous on Sunday afternoon. The sun was shining brightly as we strolled along the footpath, gazing into various cake shops before we stopped at a café and settle into seats at an outside table.

We engaged in a delightful dialogue, while I reflected on my feelings towards her. She was witty, intelligent, and reasonably attractive. However, as much as I tried to warm to her, I didn't find her sexually desirable and I couldn't help focussing on certain aspects about her that irritated me.

Dorothy had broad interests and topics for discussion, although she always seemed to gravitate back to her past. She laboured over complaints about her former boyfriends, highlighting their apparent faults and shortcomings.

I didn't know why she consistently harked back to her previous liaisons. Was she simply alerting me as to what she expected (or didn't expect) in a man? Was she attempting to tease out responses from me in order to gauge my reactions? Whatever it was, she was making me feel uncomfortable, and what had started out as a delightful conversation seemed to degenerate into an interrogation.

"I like a man who knows what he wants," Dorothy stated, and instantaneously followed up with a sharp question. "So what do you want?"

"In what respect?"

"What sort of women do you like?"

I critically pondered the question with a slightly contorted face. "I don't really have any preconceived ideas of a type of woman I like. I tend to form opinions based on my experience after I meet them and get to know them."

"Are you after a long-term relationship?"

I really felt uneasy and unsettled by this unanticipated turn of events and Dorothy's serious tone, but I attempted to answer as honestly as I could. "If I found someone I liked and who I thought would enhance my life, I'm sure I'd be open to a long-term relationship."

"Enhance your life?" she repeated. "What's that supposed to mean?"

"I always seek to improve my life and make it more enjoyable for myself and the people around me," I said as I endeavoured to express in words an accurate reflection of my true feelings. "I'd consider myself extremely lucky if I met someone who I could share my life with, who I felt comfortable with, and where we made each other happy. You know, like a soul mate."

7

"You're 40 years old and you've never had a long-term relationship," Dorothy pointed out. "I get the feeling you're incapable of making a commitment."

"I'm sure I'd be capable of committing," I replied, although it sounded somewhat unconvincing even to me.

"You've never had a long-term relationship and you've never been married," Dorothy stated in a firm voice. "Why have you never married?"

A number of thoughts pervaded my mind as I struggled with the concept of the unbreakable bond of marriage. It was a situation I had never previously considered possible for me. I then blurted out whatever words came to mind. "I guess I just haven't found the right woman yet."

My response sounded trite and I sensed that I had failed the Dorothy quiz, as she appeared unimpressed and disappointed.

I didn't feel inclined to contact Dorothy over the ensuing days, as I concluded it was unlikely we could be anything more than friends.

Nevertheless, I couldn't help reflecting on my interactions with her. She had hit a nerve with me and stirred up some innermost feelings, which instigated a serious introspection and caused flashbacks to my past life.

# Chapter 3

## My Early Years

I was born on 11 January 1961 to father Joseph, who we called Joe, and mother Mary. Although they came from the same region of Puglia in Italy, they did not meet until after they arrived in Australia.

Mary met Joe at a dance in Melbourne and, after a short courtship, they married. Although Joe once explained it to me a little differently: "I asked your mother for our first dance and she never let me go."

Joe was highly disciplinary and Mary was highly religious, although both were extremely nurturing parents.

Given my parents' strict Catholic upbringing, I was fortunate not to have been the firstborn as I was destined to be named Jesus.

As it happened, my sister came first and my parents settled on a female name they considered closest to the name Jesus: Jessica, which had the diminutive name of Jesse that was used in Spanish as a nickname for the male name of Jesus.

My parents scratched their heads when I subsequently popped out. They didn't want to call their second-born Jesus, so they followed the Italian tradition of naming me after my grandfather on my father's side, which was Francesco. The religious connection was made with San Francesco d'Assisi who was the patron saint of animals and ecology. He was also my mother's favourite saint.

My recollection of my early childhood years is as a period of absolute bliss. I was the pride of my father, being the son who could pass on the family name, and the joy of my mother, who had a burning desire for me to become a priest. Naturally, I couldn't satisfy both of them, so I thought it appropriate that I ended up disappointing both of them.

Jessica was thrilled to have a baby brother. Two years my senior, she would parade me around and show me off to everyone she knew and just about everyone we encountered.

When Jessica started getting pocket money and I was at an age when I could walk, she would bring me on short outings and treat me to cakes.

"They're one-day-old cakes," Jessica explained, regretfully. "It's all I can afford with my pocket money."

It made no difference to me as I enthusiastically devoured the treats.

It seemed that I could do no wrong. Good-natured, although highly playful and adventurous, I would invariably be a menace. What fuelled my mischievous ways was the fact that I was gently reprimanded for my misdemeanours, whereas Jessica was often held responsible for not having properly instructed and controlled me.

I was mollycoddled by Jessica, spoiled by the extended family, and pampered by family friends. It was so overwhelming and incessant I was developing a sense of privilege. It therefore came as a shock when I turned three and was despatched to be minded by Mirella, an elderly neighbour who lived down the road.

Joe worked for a manufacturing company. After Jessica started primary school, Mary commenced work in a textile factory, notwithstanding Joe's protestations that a mother should take care of the children until they went to school.

Mirella was a lovely-natured woman in her sixties whose husband had passed away many years before. Her movement was deliberate, though slow and restricted, which I suspected was due to her advanced age and her hunchback condition. She was a buxom woman who usually wore long black dresses that appeared to be framed by a cage crinoline that accentuated her rather large posterior.

During the week, Mirella's daughter and son-in-law set off for work while her grandchildren — two teenage boys — went to school. Their house was a double-fronted, four-bedroom Victorian cottage with large rooms and twelve-foot-high ceilings. The house was dark, dingy, and gloomy, with a thick atmosphere giving off a pungent potpourri odour.

Mirella took good care of me, although she struggled to juggle her childminding duties with her daily housework. One day rolled into the next and every day followed a similarly monotonous routine.

I was dropped off early in the morning to observe Mirella's family leaving for school and work. There was a cacophony of talking and movement as they collected their belongings, said their goodbyes, and rushed out. The house soon transformed from a ruckus into a morgue, with Mirella, like an undertaker, spontaneously and mechanically moving onto her tasks.

Mirella commenced in the laundry, where there appeared to be endless heaps of clothes. She sorted a portion of these into two piles. One bundle was inserted into an early-model washing machine. She then proceeded to wash a second bundle by hand with the aid of a wooden washboard.

It was lunchtime when Mirella finished hanging up the washing on the clothesline. She then gently took my hand and guided me into the kitchen where pre-prepared sandwiches and lemonade awaited us.

After lunch, Mirella escorted me into one of the bedrooms, seated me on a wooden chair, and proceeded to make the bed. I initially observed her with curiosity and was fascinated by the strange-looking bolster pillow that spanned the top of the double bed.

A little while later, I became utterly bored and, all of a sudden, a feeling of sadness came over me. My thoughts then turned to Mary. I deeply missed my mother and I impulsively shot out the room, flung open the front door, and ran up the street.

I could hear Mirella calling my name in the background as I made it home and started ringing the doorbell. There was no answer, but this did not deter me from continuing to ring.

I only stopped at the sound of Mirella's approach, when I crouched down into a ball and cried my eyes out.

Mirella arrived and took a seat beside me. After a little while, my tears subsided and I looked over at her. She gave me a wry smile and then, without a word, delicately took my hand and led me back.

# Chapter 4

## First Day of School

I was excited as I walked to school hand-in-hand with Mary on one side and Joe on the other. I wore a beaming smile as I puffed out my chest, feeling chuffed and looking resplendent in my school uniform — school tie, light-blue shirt, dark-blue pants, and dark-blue cardigan.

Sister Jane, the class teacher, greeted us. There seemed to be an official handover as Joe concluded the discussion with his parting words. "You may take charge of my son and I give you permission to discipline him."

I looked at my father, confused, not because I didn't know what he meant, but because he'd made the comment at all, particularly since my parents had never physically disciplined me.

As Sister Jane took my hand and drew me towards the classroom, I turned to watch my parents walk away. The smile was wiped off my face as my mood swung and I felt totally lost.

Sister Jane stood over a table and scanned a number of tags. She selected one and pinned it on the front of my cardigan, near my heart.

I turned up the name tag and it read 'Francis'.

"Francis? My name's not Francis; it's Frank."

"No. Your name is Francis. Your official name is Francesco, and the correct translation of Francesco into English is Francis," Sister Jane advised. "Now, I'm very busy, so run along."

It wasn't long before my name became a hot topic of conversation.

"Francis? Who has a name like Francis?" asked one boy.

"Francis is a girl's name; isn't it?" asked another boy.

"No, it is a name for a boy," suggested yet another lad. "I watch a comedy series on TV called *Francis the Talking Mule*, and the mule has a man's voice."

A horde of school kids soon joined in chorus. "He's Francis the talking mule! Francis the talking mule!"

By this time I was absolutely distraught, moisture welling in my eyes. I took a deep breath, about to burst into tears, when I was distracted by the sound of a bell, which was the call for the school children to attend class.

The rest of the morning was spent obtaining orientation information and getting to know the other students. The class was made up of an even mix of girls and boys from a variety of ethnic backgrounds.

I was relieved that none of my class members were involved in the name-calling, nor did they seem to have any issue with my name. Nevertheless, when students were given the opportunity to correct their name tags, I was quick to remonstrate that my name should be Frank.

Sister Jane remained resistant against my pleas, but I was fortunate there happened to be another Francis in the class and, to avoid confusion, she acquiesced to my request.

Hence, I became Frank again.

# Chapter 5

## Downfall of a Superhero

Over the ensuing days, months, and years, the other Francis had to endure relentless bullying; however, it wasn't his name that instigated the unwanted attention.

Francis was a short, obese boy with red hair, blue eyes, and freckles. He was a highly intelligent and creative individual, although these attributes often resulted in some fairly harsh treatment from the nastier boys.

On hot summer days, Francis would usually wear shorts, which everyone else soon learned was not a wise move. It was an open invitation for other boys to slap his legs. By the end of the day, his legs had transformed from delicate, fair skin to red raw. Even so, this did not deter him from wearing shorts and the same treatment was served out to him all over again.

Francis also had a lively imagination and would sometimes bring costumes to school, which he would change into during lunchtime. He would transform into various characters and superheroes. It was Superman one day, Batman another day, and Spiderman the next.

One day Francis dressed up as Thor, his elaborate outfit complete with a plastic helmet and hammer. This was one time when his superhuman powers were put to the test, as the get-up attracted the attention of a group of older bully boys.

"So, what do we have here?" asked one of the bullies.

"I'm Thor, of course," Francis replied.

"What's with the hammer?" asked a second bully. "You gonna build a house or something?"

"My hammer is called Mjolnir and it's an enchanted weapon with mystical powers."

"Well, we'll have to check out these mystical powers," yet another bully threatened.

As the gang closed in on Francis, a larger group of boys and girls, including myself and other children from my class, approached and tried to defend him.

"I don't want any trouble, fellas," Francis pleaded as he backed away from the gang's advance. "I'm capable of creating a powerful barrier that is impenetrable." He raised Mjolnir above his head and started to whirl it around and around in his attempt to create a vortex. "You won't be able to penetrate my powerful force field," he exclaimed.

The gang was unperturbed; they grabbed the hammer and proceeded to push Francis around.

"I'm mighty Thor!" Francis cried out.

"Yeah right," the first bully boy asserted. "You're not Thor, but you'll be mighty sore when we finish with you!"

Francis was pushed to the ground and the uproar from the crowd of school children eventually drew some nuns and lay teachers to run to his aid.

The crowd was dispersed amongst much chatter. Francis was pulled up and dusted off. He didn't seem to have any visible injuries, although his hair was dishevelled and he looked shaken. I picked up his helmet and handed it to him.

"The helmet's got a crack," I informed him.

"That's okay," Francis replied. "But where's Mjolnir?"

A thin girl with mousy, blonde hair, hazel eyes, and freckles, just like Francis, timidly approached. She was from our class and her name was Penny. She delicately handed Francis the hammer.

"Thanks Penny," Francis said as he looked into her sympathetic eyes, and they both smiled.

The bell sounded for the end of lunchtime and the students made their way back to class, while Francis made his way to the change rooms to metamorphose back into human form.

# Chapter 6

## Schoolyard Bullying

As sorry as I felt for Francis, I felt even sorrier for myself. My whole world had been turned upside down since I left my sheltered existence at home to enter the brutal environment at school.

At home I was adored, praised, and idolized, while at school I was criticized, mocked, and bullied. It was the first time in my short life that my facial disfigurements were highlighted to me, and it was done in the most savage way.

Even though I was short for my age, all my features relating to my countenance were big. What added to my distress was that the insults were based on facts; facts that, somehow, to my amazement, I had not previously noticed, nor had they ever been brought to my attention.

It was true I had a large, aquiline nose with a prominent bridge. I did have a pronounced chin. I did have a heavy brow ridge. I did have protruding ears, the condition exacerbated by the asymmetry in the extent to which they stuck out and their varied formation, with one ear having the curvature of a cauliflower and the other being flat like a pancake.

I was flabbergasted at how I'd managed to miss these striking faults, and how nobody had ever mentioned them to me before. I had obviously been living in a fool's paradise.

The name-calling and abuse occurred on a daily basis, both in the classroom and in the schoolyard. The most popular names were Big Nose, Eagle Beak, Big Ears, and Dumbo. It commenced in the early grades and became more severe over the ensuing years.

I endured the taunts as much as I could while at school and tried to mask their impact on me at home. As I now reflect on that period, I find it bewildering that, through the whole time, I never cried. However, my downbeat mood was not lost on my parents or other members of my extended family.

A few times every year, our related families would unite for festivities, with each family taking turns to host the event and the other families contributing food and drink. The gatherings comprised as many as 50 people and involved a drinking and eating extravaganza.

The next event was held at one of my aunties' houses. I was in the kitchen with my auntie and my mother where I could overhear their conversation.

"What's happened to Frank?" my auntie asked Mary, right in front of me, as if I wasn't there or wasn't listening.

"What do you mean?" Mary responded.

"He used to be so lively and boisterous; however,

21

now he seems so quiet and depressed."

"I think he's adjusting to school. I expect it's just a phase he's going through."

My mother's response did not divulge the extent of her concern, as my parents had spoken to me from time to time.

"What's wrong," Mary would ask me.

"Nothing's wrong," I would always reply. Although word that there was something wrong eventually found its way to my parents.

My parents spoke to me in the most caring manner. "You know that you're a special child," Mary repeated her frequent comment.

"I know, Ma," I said. "We are all children of God."

"Yes, that's right. And the unfortunate people of this world are those closest to God."

"I can come to school to have a word with the teachers," Joe suggested.

"No," I replied. "I don't want that."
"Maybe you could have some medical treatment," Joe said.

"No," I responded defiantly. "I don't want that either."

"We have private health insurance, so we can afford it," Joe explained.

"It's not just the money. I was born this way and therefore it's a cross I have to bear."

Mary reacted with an expression of pride and piety. Joe reacted with an assertive and compliant nod.

*　　*　　*

Mary was delighted when I made my First Confession and was about to receive my First Holy Communion, being the last of the three sacraments of Catholic initiation. She excitedly helped me put on my suit and Joe completed my attire by doing up my tie.

We had some photographs taken outside the family home before making the 10-minute walk to church. I waved to a number of my classmates and everyone was in a buoyant mood.

I kissed Jessica and my parents before I joined my fellow classmates to take a seat in church.

The mass proceeded to the point when the parishioners were to recite: "Lord, I am not worthy to receive you, but only say the word and I shall be healed."

After I said the words, I had a moment of contemplation. I queried whether I really was worthy. I hardly considered myself human, given my facial abnormalities. I often felt that, unlike any other human, animal, or living being, I didn't deserve my place in the world. I sometimes wondered why I'd ever been born at all.

I then reflected on my mother's words, that the unfortunate people were closest to God, and I opened my praying hands to marvel at my palms, which were bright pink with a shiny, smooth texture that appeared pure.

I was seated at the end of the first pew. The students in my row stood and reverently moved towards the sanctuary as the priest positioned himself to give Holy Communion. I followed them and stood in line, waiting patiently.

It didn't take long before I was standing in front of the priest, and I heard him say, "The body of Christ."

"Amen," I proudly responded.

The priest placed the host on my tongue and I returned to my seat. I knelt down and placed my palms together to assume a 'prayer hands' position while I mused over the experience. I felt complete.

At the end of the service, the parishioners made their way outside and there was much socialising, with a festive atmosphere. We leisurely strolled to the school where a celebration party was set up in the main hall.

It was a high-spirited affair with a good time had by all. I was joyful during the event, and when I saw the smiles on the faces of Mary, Joe, and Jessica, I was euphoric.

\*　　\*　　\*

Most of the teachers were good to me, although there was one nun, Sister Heloise, who, for some reason, treated me harshly.

Sister Heloise was a strict and most-feared teacher who always carried around a cane. She would often whack it against a desk or other hard object that would give off a loud cracking sound, which was threatening and intimidating.

During one of Sister Heloise's classes, she was extremely stroppy. A couple of boys behind me were taking turns in kicking me. I turned around and whispered for them to stop. Sister Heloise noticed, came hurtling towards me, and cracked the top of my desk with her cane. Everyone in class was stunned to attention.

"You should not be chattering in class," Sister Heloise told me. "I want you to meet me in this room after school."

I was horrified, as I had never been reprimanded before, and I took a moment before I replied, "Yes, Sister Heloise."

At the end of school, I attended the class and Sister Heloise was waiting for me.

"I want you to take out your pen and paper, and write out for me 500 times 'I must not talk in class'."

"Yes, Sister Heloise."

"When you finish you can go home, but make sure to close the door behind you," Sister Heloise instructed, and then she left, closing the door behind her.

I looked around the room that was in eerie silence. I then got to work, writing 'I must not talk in class' over and over and over. There were 40 lines per page and I wrote the verse twice on each line. After 6 pages, I wrote it a final 20 times. I confirmed my arithmetic before I made to set off.

I got to the door and tried to release the latch, but I couldn't. I tried again, but it simply would not give way. I was getting frustrated and had a rest. I pondered the situation and reflected on how I was on the third floor and, therefore, couldn't exit through a window.

I recommenced my attack on the latch, but to no avail. I then commenced banging on the door and calling out. "Hello? I need help. I can't get out. Please help me."

I felt forlorn and helpless as my thoughts turned to my family who I knew would be waiting for me. In my desperation, I started to cry and renewed my calls for help.

After a while, I heard a familiar voice and recognised it as my father's.

"I'm in here," I called out.

I heard a loud click as the latch released. The door swung open and there stood Joe, Mary, and Jessica. Mary was crying as she took me in her arms and hugged me. Jessica joined in the hug, while Joe examined the door.

"Go outside and close the door," Joe instructed us. We did so, and soon heard tinkering noises around the latch. "Okay, open the door."

Jessica released the latch from the outside and opened the door.

"The door doesn't open from the inside," Joe said. "Frank, I'm coming with you to school tomorrow to have a word with the teacher."

True to his word, the next day Joe escorted me to school and demanded to speak to Sister Heloise. The headmistress, Sister Theresa, accompanied us.

"Did you leave my son in the classroom yesterday after school?" Joe asked Sister Heloise.

"Your son was very naughty, so I taught him a lesson," she replied.

"Did you leave my son in the classroom alone?" Joe assertively repeated his question.

"Yes, I did; however, I told him he could leave after he had completed his task. I didn't know the latch was jammed from inside the room."

"The fact is, you were responsible for my son and you left him alone and unsupervised, which is wrong. I do not want anything like this to happen again."

Joe looked sternly at Sister Heloise before he turned to Sister Theresa. Neither of them had anything to say. He then turned to me and gave me a reassuring nod.

# Chapter 7

## Puberty Blues

On weekends, I would habitually join a group of girls and boys from the neighbourhood to go down to the nearby creek to play. The creek had a rocky cliff face on one side and thick vegetation on the other.

We would engage in numerous activities, from catching frogs, to climbing the cliff, and floating on our self-made wooden raft.

One day, as I was on my way home, I came across a large yellow envelope without any writing or markings. I broke the seal to reveal a magazine and a novel. I placed the envelope under my arm and headed home.

When I reached my bedroom, I opened the envelope and took out the magazine. I turned the pages, and it contained photographic images of two young women, fully nude, in various poses and physical interactions. I was confused by the images, so I sought out Jessica to ask her about them.

I knocked on Jessica's bedroom door and she told me to enter. She was lying on her bed, reading a book, and I jumped on the bed next to her.

"I found this magazine down the creek and I don't

know what it's about."

Jessica flipped through the pages, expressionless. "They look like two young ladies exploring and enjoying each other's bodies," she casually explained.

"That's what I thought, because they both look happy. Do all girls do that?" I innocently asked.

Jessica smiled. "No, not all girls. Usually girls like boys and boys like girls."

"Who do you like?"

"I like boys. Has Dad spoken to you about the birds and the bees?"

"The what?"

"I think I might have a word with him."

I left the magazine with Jessica and returned to my room. I emptied the envelope and the novel was the only remaining item, which I placed in my desk drawer.

I couldn't sleep one night as I tossed and turned. I then remembered the novel. I switched on my reading light and collected the book. It was missing the front cover and I couldn't make out what it was about, but I just started reading.

The book told the story of two schoolgirls embarking on a beach holiday with their respective parents. The girls had both recently turned 18 and were best of friends. Their minds seemed obsessively monopolised with thoughts of sex.

Melanie was described as tall and slim, with silky blonde hair, green eyes, and shapely long legs. Ruth was described as a voluptuous girl with wavy dark hair and blue eyes. Both were depicted as being attractive in their own way.

What amazed me about the descriptions was that they matched the two girls I'd seen in the magazine. As a consequence, the two characters came alive in my imagination and the story became more vivid, almost as if I had become a part of the book.

After the initial scene-setting, even though I felt the story was lifelike, it dragged on. My interest was only maintained by the occasional expletive words, such as cunt, prick, anus, and breast; words I had never previously seen written, other than in graffiti.

I completed a few chapters before I grew tired, returned the book to my desk, and went to sleep.

The following night, I was restless and kept thinking about the book. I eventually got up and continued reading.

The two girls frolicked through the lavender fields. A cool breeze raised Ruth's light floral dress above her knees, which stimulated her as she wasn't wearing any panties. The bright sunlight beamed through her dress so the shape of her body was silhouetted. Her legs were spread and you could follow the outline of her inner thighs to the point where the lines were lost in her hairy bush. Giggling, they rushed back to her bedroom and she moved in front of the mirror. Ruth grabbed Melanie's skirt frill and pulled her dress over her head, removing it and throwing it on the floor. Admiring Melanie's shapely, slender body, Ruth commenced to cup her breasts, before she slid her hands down her body, between her legs, and felt the fire.

As I read the passage I had a titillating sensation in my penis. Even though I felt uncomfortable and embarrassed, I forced myself to finish the chapter and then put the book away.

The following night, I lay in bed contemplating whether I should continue reading the book. I had mixed feelings: inquisitiveness on the one hand and apprehension on the other. In the end, curiosity got the better of me and I continued with the next chapter.

Returning from an afternoon swim at the beach, the two girls entered the change rooms and Ruth stripped off her swimsuit. Melanie felt a tingle of excitement as she admired Ruth's nudity and was captivated by her smooth, rounded buttocks. Melanie felt exhilarated and got the urge to undress as well.

I stopped reading to take a breath. I was starting to get the arousal feelings of the night before, but I felt compelled to continue.

The two girls invited the middle-aged man to join them. They undressed him and stood back to examine his drooping, hairy body. Ruth took his penis in her hand and stroked it. He felt his prick hardening and she took it in her mouth. The girls made him lie down as they undressed and climbed on top of him. He gently caressed their bodies, cupping their breasts and pinching their nipples. He ran his cold, wet tongue up and down their bodies. He took Ruth's breast in his mouth, gently bit on her nipple, and sucked on it. He was highly excited and devoured whatever was presented to him — a mouth, a breast, a vagina. His cool fingers sent a shiver down Melanie's back. He was kissing her salty-tasting mouth when he felt a warm, wet vagina engulf his hard cock. They took turns in mounting him. Ruth gyrated her torso on top of him and groaned with delight as she grinded away, rocking back and forth. He assumed a dominant position and took her from behind. She could feel his hot, heavy breath on the back of her neck. Her moans increased as she grabbed hold of the pillow. He desired to feel every inch of her flesh and grabbed hold of her fists. They squeezed their bodies in unison in a futile attempt to maintain the moment. Ruth could not control her emotions as her body quivered and shook. Melanie lay flat on her back and waited for him to engulf her. His hard member tickled her cunt. As she felt his penis against her vagina, she drew him closer in an effort to thrust his prick into her. He eventually succumbed, allowing his cock to infiltrate her body. She rose to meet him as she groaned with ecstasy, and he drove himself deeper into her.

To my astonishment, as I read the climactic end to the chapter, I felt stimulation to my erogenous zones I previously didn't even know existed, and I experienced an overwhelming penile arousal. I attempted to squeeze my groin in an effort to control and subdue the sensations; however, it progressed to the point where my penis began pulsating, oozing a warm, gooey, clear liquid that spread over my pyjamas.

I carefully got out of bed and dragged myself to the bathroom, holding my pyjamas away from my body. I washed myself in the bidet Joe had fitted, even though he said it was for the ladies, which had completely baffled me.

I returned to bed, lay on my back, and contemplated what had just happened. It took some time before I learned I had had my first orgasm.

*     *     *

I became more aware of unusual sights and smells regarding the physiology of the primary school girls and boys. The more obvious example was the school children's physical growth. A more unpleasant condition that I picked up on, which I found most curious, was that girls often smelt like pee and the boys often smelt like poo.

There was one boy in particular who habitually gave off the stink of excrement. His name was Luca and he was frequently berated for his foul smell. During the summer months, flies swarmed around his rear end. While many students cracked jokes about it behind his back, I tried to be helpful by bringing it to his attention.

"Luca, do you know you smell of shit?" I bluntly asked him.

"I don't smell of shit, but it sounds like you're talking shit."

"I'm telling you as a friend, because a lot of the kids make fun of you."

"I don't know what you're talking about."

"Well, why do you think you have all those flies buzzing around your arse?"

"I guess they like me."

*    *    *

There were noticeable changes in my physiology when I turned 10. I presented with early stages of puberty, the most obvious changes being facial pimples and my voice starting to break, which gained me a broad following of laughing students.

During an English class, the teacher instructed me to read from a book. It was a challenging passage, although it normally would not have caused me any trouble.

As I proceeded, my voice started to break, which caused instantaneous chuckles from a couple of students. I continued, and my voice increasingly cracked, with more of the students commencing to giggle. It got to the point where my voice was breaking regularly and all the students were laughing. I was distraught and stopped reading, looking up at the teacher.

The teacher was following the passage from his copy of the book, and when he noted I had stopped reading, he glanced over. "Please continue," he said.

I reluctantly recommenced reading, with my voice continuing to break and the students continuing to laugh.

After what I felt to be an eternity, the teacher instructed me to stop. I took a deep breath of relief as the sounds of the students' laughter and chatter lingered.

Mathematics was my favourite subject, and the

teacher sometimes conducted times tables speed contests whereby students were pitted against each other in the form of a knockout competition. Two at a time, students would stand at the back of the room, the teacher would call out numbers, and the quickest student to bark the answer would take a step forward.

The next contest was organised and I cruised through the first few rounds. As the contest intensified, my voice started to crack under the pressure, making all sorts of odd noises, which reached a crescendo as we approached the final stages of the contest.

"Six sevens," the teacher called out.

"Forty-two," I replied in a loud whine, and took another step forward, one step away from the blackboard at the front of the room, while the girl in the final was only about halfway.

The sounds emanating from my voice initially gained giggles from the other students, but, by this time, they grew into belly laughter.

"Eleven twelves," the teacher shouted, in order to be heard above the noise.

"One hundred and thirty-two," I tried to shout as my voice creaked, cracked, and petered out in an involuntary yodel.

By this time the class was in pandemonium and even the teacher could not contain her laughter.

I won the contest and was awarded a packet of lollies, which I raised triumphantly into the air. Overtly I was jubilant, but covertly I was devastated.

# Chapter 8

## A Targeted Attack

Changes in my physiology due to puberty caused a bit of a growth spurt and I was now of average height among the boys in my class, as well as being physically stronger. The downside was it resulted in the development of facial hair and the worsening of my pimples.

Primary school threw up many surprises and I began to fear what the next day would bring. Whereas I would normally be lambasted about my abnormal facial features or the breaking of my voice, I now had to contend with further challenges.

My history of being bullied on a regular basis had developed into normalcy, although the emergence of my puberty seemed to up the ante. I was now gaining more physical attention from the older, sixth-grade bullies. There were four or five who gave me a hard time, but there was one boy, named Blake, who took a particular disliking towards me.

Blake was tall and strong. He had light-brown hair and blue eyes. He was the leader of one of the two main gangs at the school, referred to as the Aussie gang. The Aussie gang mainly comprised boys of Irish

Catholic descent.

The other main gang was known as the Wog gang. Wog being a derogatory term that referred to continental Europeans. The Wog gang mainly comprised Catholic boys from Italian ethnicity and it was led by a big, strong individual named Bruno.

One day, after the bell had sounded for the end of lunchtime, I was heading to class when Blake and three of his cronies cut me off and pinned me to a fence.

Blake waited until the schoolyard was vacated before he turned his attention to me. "So, Francis, you really do irritate just about everyone," he said. "You're ugly, you've got no friends, everybody hates you, and you don't belong to any gang. I just don't know why you bother coming to this school at all."

I just returned his stare and didn't say a word.

"Cat got your tongue?" one of the boys remarked.

I still didn't speak, and Blake then punched me in the guts. I hunched over, badly winded. I was held up by the cronies while another boy took his turn in punching me. On this occasion, I was prepared, and I tensed for the blow. This was followed by the other two boys taking their turns.

"We don't want to see you at this school anymore," Blake viciously yelled. "Okay guys, let's tie him up."

Astonished, I looked up at them. "What are you doing?"

"Oh, he's talking now," one of the boys said.

They forced me over to one of the poles on the basketball court. I tried to resist, but I was overpowered. They roughly grabbed my arms, raised my hands above my head, and tied my wrists to the pole.

"Whenever you get loose, I want you to get out of this school, and make sure you never come back," Blake said sternly with a grim smile.

The gang went inside the school building and I was left languishing on the pole.

I just stood there for a little while, sensing I somehow deserved the punishment for being who I was. I then considered that I couldn't stay there for the rest of the day, so I attempted to free myself.

I tried to wriggle out of the ropes, but they were fastened tightly. I was becoming concerned as, even though I knew I would eventually be liberated, I didn't want the ignominy of being found in this situation.

I became more desperate and vigorously writhed in various directions. It must have taken almost an hour before I managed to free myself, my wrists bloodied and bruised.

I went to the boys' bathroom and washed my hands, wrists, and arms. It was still more than an hour before the end of school, but I didn't want to go to class in my condition, so I just walked the streets. I arrived home when I was due and went through my normal routine without telling anyone what had happened.

The next day, I returned to school.

*   *   *

There was no let-up to the name-calling and bullying. In fact, it seemed to get more intense and aggressive. I did my best to ignore the unwanted attention and to hide the personal hurt it caused me at school and at home.

A sense of worthlessness was preoccupying my mind. I felt like my physical being was just taking up space in the world. I saw no end to my dire situation, and the pressure and stress on me was growing. I reached a level of frustration where I commenced to undertake silly and irrational action.

I made a point of sleeping on my sides, making sure my ears were pinned back against my head. When I was wet with perspiration, my ears sometimes stuck momentarily to my head before they sprang back out.

I then started using band-aids to stick my ears against my head before I went to bed, but this didn't hold either.

In a drastic step, I applied super glue to the back of my ears, although I found out that wasn't such a good idea either. When I got up the next morning, the super glue caused a burning effect, taking away several layers of skin, and my ears popped out, just like before.

In my desperation, I once held a utility knife as I

looked in the mirror and contemplated the idea of cutting off my ears. I was never actually going to do it, as it would have been a breach of my religious faith in not being prepared to carry my cross. I also knew it would have devastated my family.

Whatever ideas I thought of or action I took, I couldn't come up with any practical measures to address my situation, nor could I remedy the pain I felt.

# Chapter 9

## School Gangs

I had reached sixth grade and joined one of the school's two senior classes. As it had been every year, this meant there was recruiting of gang members and jockeying for the position of gang leader.

The new leader of the Wog gang was John and the new leader of the Aussie gang was Sean.

John was a tough guy who was well known to the police as he had been arrested many times. He was a loose cannon and his unpredictability struck fear into the hearts of students, teachers, and gang members alike.

Sean was of Irish descent and a real fireball. He had a fetish for boxing, which was urged on by his father, who was an amateur boxer in his own right.

John and Sean had a healthy respect for each other, which resulted in a reasonably harmonious environment within the school. They also kept the smaller gangs and individual toughies in check. On the other hand, they created havoc outside school, which resulted in many visits from the police.

I had been marginalised and was never involved in any of the gangs, nor did I have any interest in becoming so involved. I was generally left alone, although I was pushed around by members of both gangs and, on occasion, by other tough guys. The students in general seemed content to call me names — something I had grown used to.

At the time when the gangs were being reconstituted, the gang members sniffed around to gain new recruits.

There were various points in the schoolyard where boys challenged others to join their desired gang. This involved a lot of tough-talking, skirmishes, and fights.

The boys looked like mini gladiators as they pitted their skills against each other. John and Sean observed the action from their respective vantage points, like two emperors.

I was with one of my closest classmates, Robert, observing the developments with bemusement, when two deputies of the Aussie gang and a prospective recruit turned their attention to us.

"What are you looking at?" one of the deputies asked.

"Nothing," Robert replied.

"You must be looking at something," the other deputy stated. "So what are you looking at?"

"We're just hanging out," I said. "We're not really looking at anything in particular."

"This guy's just a smart arse," the first deputy told the prospective recruit. "I want you to bash him up."

"No problem," the prospective recruit responded as he pulled up his sleeves and rushed towards me. I averted his advance and manoeuvred around his punches.

"Fight him, you scaredy-cat!" the second deputy shouted to me.

"I'm not fighting anyone!"

"If you don't fight him we're going to bash up your little friend," the first deputy threatened as he grabbed Robert by the hair with one hand and the scruff of his neck with the other, and shook him around like a rag doll.

Robert gave a loud scream.

"All right!" I yelled.

"Good," the first deputy said. "The rules are that anything goes and the fight goes on until one guy decks the other guy. Any questions?"

There were no questions, and the prospective recruit started bouncing around and shadowboxing. He was roughly my height, but a bit chubby. I could tell he had no idea how to fight, as he tried to punch me with the flats of his hands, more of a slap, and he swung wildly without much control.

I had never been involved in a fight before, but my father, who had served in the Italian navy and was trained in boxing, had given me a few pointers for self defence. I just moved around the prospective recruit's advances as he became tired and frustrated.

"Come on, you guys," the second deputy called out. "Get on with it!"

I walked forward, dodged a left hook, and, while he was unbalanced, launched into a right-hand haymaker punch, which connected flush on his cheek and floored him. He was only mildly dazed and soon jumped up to continue the fight; however, the rules of the contest meant it was over.

"Let's go," I told Robert and we walked off.

Sean observed the events with a firm stare, and John looked on with a smirk.

*    *    *

Weeks later, there was a game of volleyball being played at lunchtime in the schoolyard and the opposing teams were broadly made up of the Aussie gang and the Wog gang.

The competition was fierce, with a number of disagreements and hostilities. There were arguments at the end of almost every point. The deciding set was a close contest, with players and members of the crowd losing their temper, and it quickly developed into a brawl.

Teachers came from all directions to intervene, but although they were able to temporarily subdue the ruckus, they were unable to settle the argument and the melee looked set to recommence.

The referees asked a number of gang members whether the ball fell in or out, but they were not believed by one side or the other. The referees then asked some of the non-partisan crowd, but they either replied that they didn't see the ball or that they didn't know.

Sean then spotted me. "Why don't we ask Frank?"

I was universally considered as someone who was incapable of lying.

John was holding someone by the collar, but he pushed him away and walked towards me. "Yeah, why don't we ask Frank?"

I was lying back on my elbows in a nonchalant manner.

"Well, Frank," one of the referees said. "Did you see the ball and, if so, was it in or out?"

"Yeah, I saw the ball," I replied as the crowd massed around me. "I thought the ball was out."

John took an aggressive step towards me, then stopped in his tracks and took a hard look at me. I simply returned his stare in a calm, expressionless way.

"Fair enough," John said. "You guys win this time."

The concession settled the matter and the winning side erupted in celebration while the losing side walked off.

# Chapter 10

## The New Headmistress

Early 1972, during sixth grade, Sister Theresa departed the school and was replaced as headmistress by a new nun named Sister Brenda. In addition, two new lay teachers were employed.

The two lay teachers comprised a female teacher, named Barbara, and a male physical education teacher, named Todd. The two were very chummy and rumours were rife they were having an affair. They also got on well with Sister Brenda.

The introduction of the new entrants changed the dynamics of the teaching staff. Barbara and Todd acted like interlopers, with the other teachers appearing more subdued, except for Sister Heloise, who elevated the level of her viciousness.

I never came into contact with Barbara; however, I had physical education classes with Todd on a weekly basis.

Todd always appeared to have a smile on his face and often giggled, seemingly finding humour in anything and everything. He looked fit and healthy, although he acted lazy with a laidback teaching style. He usually shouted instructions from his fold-up chair and ran various gymnastic competitions.

Todd also had some odd habits. One was when the class was too loud or disorganised for his liking and he would order everyone to sit on the floor, if we were in the gymnasium, or on the ground, if we were in the schoolyard.

"This class is too disobedient," Todd would say with a smile. "So, I think we should send a few of you to the headmistress to be disciplined."

Todd would then stand up and spin his body in a whirl with a straightened arm and pointed index finger. When he stopped, he would pick out a student.

"You're the one," Todd would tell them. "I want you to go to Sister Brenda and tell her I sent you to her because you'd been misbehaving."

Todd repeated this process a few times, and as the boys and girls were selected, they would walk off as ordered.

I, like the rest of the class, was dumbfounded by this practice and fearful of being selected. However, as time went on, it was generally suspected that those selected were favoured students who did not get disciplined at all. Rather, they were relieved of having to play any further part in the gymnastics class.

I was good at gymnastics and featured in the finals of many competitions. Even so, I didn't seem to find myself in Todd's good books, although I was comforted I didn't get on his bad side. On the other hand, I now often found myself in trouble with Sister

Heloise and, at times, with Sister Brenda.

Sister Heloise would pull me up on the most trivial and contrived charges, such as talking too much, disturbing other students, or being out of uniform. Most other students acted in a similar, or even worse, way; however, they didn't feel her wrath.

Whereas Sister Heloise gave detention and writing-based punishment to young students, the seniors generally got corporal punishment. It was usually two strikes with the cane on the buttocks or a leather strap on the hands for misdemeanours, and up to six strikes for more serious transgressions.

As odd as I found Sister Heloise, I thought Sister Brenda to be even stranger. In fact, I considered Sister Brenda bizarre. She would be found prancing up and down the corridors emitting a high-pitched cackle — laughing like a witch.

I did my best to avoid Sister Brenda, although I was not always successful. On one occasion, I was walking down the corridor on my way to class when I stumbled upon a group of younger students. I then noticed Sister Brenda in the middle of the group. As I couldn't make my way through, I waited for the way to clear.

Sister Brenda had a bag full of individually wrapped lollies under her left arm and she was throwing the lollies in the air with her right hand.

The students were going berserk, trying to catch the lollies in the air, or scrounging them off the floor. I was transfixed by the scene, feeling like I was in a twilight zone. As soon as I saw there was some room for me to pass, I tried to sidle through.

Unfortunately, Sister Brenda caught sight of me and I of her. She then moved down the corridor, towards her office, as she threw the remaining lollies in the air and commenced her sinister, witch-like laugh, which echoed down the corridor. I stood there momentarily in disbelief.

I joined the class and, soon after, I was advised by Sister Heloise that Sister Brenda wished to see me. The smile on Sister Heloise's face as she told me signified it could not be good.

I approached Sister Brenda's office and knocked on the door.

"Come," Sister Brenda said in a melodious voice and, when she saw me, she told me to enter and close the door.

"Francis, or is it Frank? No matter, whatever it is. I understand you often misbehave in class and have been a handful for poor Sister Heloise. It's unfortunate you do not seem to learn your lesson. It is therefore disappointing to have seen you loitering in the corridors rather than being in class."

I felt I should try to make a defence; however, Sister Brenda seemed to be on a mission and I didn't want to upset her agenda.

"Therefore, I feel it is my responsibility to discipline you. Would you like to be strapped on your left hand or your right? I guess you write with your right hand, so it may be wise that we use your left."

Sister Brenda walked to her desk, unlocked a drawer, and pulled out a leather strap. She then approached me, freed her arms from her habit, and straightened her arm with the strap in her hand.

For some reason, I wasn't frightened. In fact, I felt no emotion and acted robotically. I raised my left hand until it met the leather strap.

Sister Brenda raised her arm until it was straight up, high in the air, and whacked it down. She caught my hand flush, although I hardly felt much pain. She repeated the act three more times. I was about to leave when she interrupted me.

"Where do you think you're going," she said in a nervous voice. "I haven't finished with you yet."

I sensed that maybe she was annoyed I hadn't shown any pain or emotion. She raised the strap again and I raised my left hand. She seemed to put in a strenuous effort and whacked down once again. On this occasion, she caught my fingertips and it stung. This caused me to grimace and squeeze the tips of my fingers, which put a smile on her face. She gave me one more strap, which hurt a little. With the six straps completed, so was my punishment.

"I hope you've learned your lesson," Sister Brenda said. "Because I'm going to keep an eye on you for the remainder of this year and all of next year."

I walked out the room utterly confounded, as there were only a few days left in the year and I already knew I had passed grade six, so I wouldn't be at the school the next year.

I felt I should have advised Sister Brenda of her misconceptions; however, as I hadn't said anything throughout the meeting, I didn't see any reason to open my mouth now.

I had a passing thought as I made my way back to class, about how I had progressed through all of primary school and, notwithstanding the name-calling, bullying, and corporal punishment, I had always maintained above-average assessments, achieving A's and B's in all my subjects. In fact, I wondered whether I had found a safe haven and refuge from all my troubles through academia.

I returned to class and took my seat. I suspected Sister Heloise knew that I got the strap, so when she grinned and I reacted with a broad, glowing smile, she was bowled over.

# Chapter 11

## Secondary School

I was relieved to leave primary school and happy that a number of my school friends were to attend the same all-boys secondary school run by Christian brothers. The school was situated about three kilometres from my house, which was accessible via public transport in the form of a bus travelling two kilometres east and a tram travelling one kilometre south. Alternatively, one could walk the distance in roughly the same time.

On the first day of secondary school, I joined two of my friends — Lou and Michael — to undertake the 30-minute walk. Lou was a friend from primary school and Michael became my friend since his family had recently moved into the neighbourhood.

When we arrived at the school, we were allocated to our classes, with Michael and Lou going to Form 1 Blue while I ended up in Form 1 Gold.

Brother Mahoney, our first teacher, introduced himself. He was a tall, thin, middle-aged man with a stunned expression. He took the attendance and provided some information about the school before he excused himself and left the room.

We were placed in single-unit, double-seater wooden desks with a bench seat. Each of the two students who shared the desks had a hinged desktop that opened to a compartment to store their belongings.

I was seated next to Reno, a boy I didn't know. We were talking, as were most of the other students in the room, when Brother Mahoney returned.

"Were you talking?" Brother Mahoney asked Reno in a blasé manner.

"No, Brother," he promptly answered.

I looked at Reno in bewilderment. *You liar.*

Brother Mahoney took a couple of steps towards the platform, then stopped and looked at me. "Were you talking?" he asked in a matter-of-fact way.

"Yes, Brother," I automatically answered.

"Really," Brother Mahoney said, seemingly surprised by my honest response. "Well, come up here then."

I followed Brother Mahoney onto the platform. He picked up a leather strap from his desk and straightened his arm out.

"Raise your hand," he instructed.

I slowly raised my right hand and, at the moment it reached the desired level, Brother Mahoney instinctively raised his arm to the ceiling and whacked it down in one rapid motion.

The strap met my hand flush and let off a loud clapping sound, which was instantaneously followed by oohs and aahs from the students.

Excruciating pain shot through my hand and I reacted by clenching it, holding it tight with my left hand and cradling both against my chest as I crouched over.

"Okay, raise your other hand," Brother Mahoney said.

I straightened defiantly as I wiggled the fingers on my right hand and raised my left. Brother Mahoney repeated his highly efficient and effective strap motion, which was followed by the sound of a loud clap and more oohs and aahs. I crouched over, as I had done the first time, although the second strap had been even more vicious than the first and I took a little longer to recover.

"I don't approve of students talking without permission in my class," Brother Mahoney advised. "So I hope you have all learned a lesson."

I spent most of the remainder of the morning mulling over the incident and trying to come to terms with it.

As the bell signified lunchtime, the class was dismissed. I was one of the last students to leave the room and, as I made it to the schoolyard and took a seat on one of the benches, I was greeted by a number of students with comments of support.

I was heartened by the comments; however, as I joined a few of the boys to play 'down ball', the name-calling started.

Upon returning to class, I was on my best behaviour.

After school, I joined Michael and Lou for the walk home and we discussed the events of the day. From what we could gauge, the teachers seemed to make examples of certain students at the beginning of every year in order to pull everyone into line from the outset.

On the second day, I was relieved to survive the morning classes unscathed. I was in the corridor at my locker retrieving the books for my next class, when I dropped one of them and unthinkingly said, "Bloody hell."

One of the lay teachers, Mr Nassar, happened to be walking by and exclaimed in a loud, firm voice, "How dare you swear!"

I was taken by surprise and confused by the accusation. "I didn't swear," I replied.

"How can you talk back to me in that manner?" Mr Nassar asked with a serious expression. "You swear and then try to deny it by arguing with a teacher!" He pinched my cheek while he shook his arm, then led me by the arm to his office.

I knew very well what was in store and I had just one thought: *Bloody hell*. However, rather than a strap, Mr Nassar took out a cane from the cupboard. "Bend over," he instructed.

Mr Nassar struck me four times on my bottom. It hurt, but nowhere near as painful as the strap dealt out by Brother Mahoney.

I was subsequently late for class and it happened to be with Brother Mahoney. The door was closed and I looked through the window to see all the students seated. When they saw me, some shook their heads, some smiled, and others both smiled and shook their heads.

I momentarily didn't know what to do, but then resigned myself to the fact that I had to enter the classroom. I tried to open the door, but it was locked, so I knocked.

Brother Mahoney stopped writing on the blackboard, turned around, and slowly walked over. He unlocked the door, cracked it open, and poked his head through. "Can I help you?" he asked.

"I'm sorry, Brother, but I'm late for class."

He looked at me with his usual stunned expression. "You should have been on time; the class is closed now. I'll see you tomorrow." He then closed the door.

I had not anticipated this course of events. In fact, even now they had transpired, I still couldn't believe them. I spent the hour reading in the library before attending my remaining classes. I then took the long walk home alone. All that while, and throughout the night, I contemplated my meeting with Brother Mahoney the following day, which loomed in my mind like a large, black cloud.

In the morning, I walked to school with Lou and Michael. I apprised them of what had occurred the previous day and they didn't say much, other than to wish me luck.

I was on time for my first class, which was with

Brother Mahoney. I was on tenterhooks, but no mention of the day before came up. During the course of the day, I was preoccupied with thoughts about my last class, which was also with Brother Mahoney, and I had enormous difficulty concentrating on anything else.

It was taking an eternity, but the time for the last class eventually ticked over. I was one of the first students to be seated, with the others arriving at regular intervals. Brother Mahoney was the last to enter and proceeded with the class until the bell rang. The class was dismissed and I remained seated until the last few students were making their way out, at which time, I began to leave.

"Frank," Brother Mahoney said. "You can stay."

I stopped and took a deep breath as I looked to the heavens.

"We have unfinished business from yesterday," Brother Mahoney recalled. "Some students take longer to learn lessons than others, but I think you'll get there in the end."

Brother Mahoney walked to his desk and picked up the leather strap. I placed my books down and clenched my fists. He walked across the platform and positioned himself. I crossed in front of him and, without him saying a word, raised my right hand.

Brother Mahoney lined up the strap and stood stationary for a while. I was anticipating the strike and wondered what he was waiting for when he raised his arm and whacked it down in a flash.

The strap met my hand flush and let off a loud clapping sound, just like before. The pain was agonising, as extreme and piercing as the first time. I clenched my right hand.

"Okay, raise your hand," Brother Mahoney said. I began to raise my left hand when he stopped me. "No, let's stick to the right hand."

I raised my right hand again, which was still smarting from the first strap. Brother Mahoney didn't procrastinate this time and he routinely whacked the strap down. Again, contact was flush.

Unlike the first strap, on this occasion I gave out a yelp as I clenched my hand, which was radiating compounding and extreme pain. I held it with my other hand and felt it pulsating as I cradled both hands close to my chest, rocking my upper body.

"You can leave when you feel up to it," Brother Mahoney said, and he departed.

I had an unsettled night with little sleep. In the morning, I mechanically went through my routine in getting ready before joining Michael and Lou for the walk to school.

Again, I briefed them on the events of the previous day. They looked concerned, as they had managed to avoid all forms of punishment. Again, they wished me luck.

I attended my classes one after the other without any repercussions; however, I knew the one after lunch was with Brother Mahoney. I had lunch on my own and turned up to class early. It went smoothly and finished without incident, so I felt more comfortable.

I was buoyed when it came to my final class with Brother O'Brien. Nearing the end of the day, many of the students were restless and became unruly. Brother O'Brien attempted to quieten them; however, it seemed to trigger a rebellion, and they became chaotic.

"Enough!" Brother O'Brien shouted above the noise, which silenced the students. "As first-year students, I understand you may not be used to the expected behaviour at this school; however, you are secondary school students who should know better, and this form of behaviour is unacceptable."

The students looked at each other, seemingly confused. I had been seated and quiet the whole time and, as such, didn't pay too much mind to what was going on; however, my level of interest was soon to change.

"I want everyone to line up along the walls," Brother O'Brien said.

The students lined up, with expressions of surprise and murmurings of confusion. Bewildered, I joined them.

Brother O'Brien walked to his desk and pulled out a leather strap. He then centred himself on the platform and summoned the boy at the head of the line to come forward. There were around 30 boys in the class and each of us received two straps, one on each hand.

Brother O'Brien commenced with some vigour and I was tenth in line. It was a firm strap, although I only felt a little pain. As he reached the final few students, he was just about worn out, and the straps appeared to be not much more than a tap. By the time the last student resumed his seat, the bell sounded and we were dismissed for the day.

I walked to school with Michael and Lou on Friday morning. We were in a good mood, being as it was the last day of the school week.

I attended my first class with Brother Smith and my second with Brother O'Brien, both classes going smoothly. It was the best day I had spent at the school so far and I felt content as I set off for lunch in high spirits.

I was elated to have met up with Carlo from primary school and we ate lunch together. We started to muck around, and Carlo challenged me to a game of 'tiggy off the ground'.

Carlo was 'it', so I ran off and he was in quick pursuit. He almost caught up with me, but I managed to jump over the veranda railings. I was airborne when he tagged me, so I was safe and he continued the pursuit. As I was climbing some steps, I tripped and fell. He was almost upon me when we were both picked up by the arm.

It was Brother Mahoney and he pulled us up off the ground. He grabbed Carlo by the ear with one hand and me by the ear with the other. He then led us along the corridor.

"What do you boys think you're doing? Your parents spend hard-earned money to buy your uniforms and you repay them by rolling around on the ground, dirtying and ruining your clothes."

Brother Mahoney left Carlo in a classroom, instructing him to stay there, and led me farther along the corridor into the next classroom.

Brother Mahoney was dressed in full clerical garb. He pulled out a leather strap from somewhere in the lining of his clothing, as if he was unsheathing a sword, and placed it on a desk. He removed his black cassock, carefully folded it, and placed it on another desk. He then removed a set of brown rosary beads and respectfully placed them on top of the cassock. It appeared as though he was following some form of ritual. Finally, he removed his white clerical tab and placed it on the desk on top of the cassock. He then picked up the strap and turned to me.

"I think you know the drill."

I stepped onto the platform and raised my right hand. Brother Mahoney followed his usual routine, whacking down, the strap crashing flush with my hand, sparking excruciating pain, which caused me to automatically clench my fist. After a few moments, I looked up to see him waiting for me, calmly swinging the strap by his side.

"Will the second one be on the right hand or the left?" I asked.

"Let's stick to the right."

I raised my right hand and he gave it another

almighty whack. I could almost predict the phases of extreme, compounding pain as I clenched and released my hand in a futile effort to relieve the dreadful soreness. I was taking my time, thinking that was the extent of the punishment I had to endure; however, I was mistaken.

"Come on. We don't have all day. Carlo is waiting for me," Brother Mahoney advised. "Raise your right hand again."

Realising my mistake in assuming that I was going to get the standard two straps added further misgivings and, as I stepped onto the platform again, I felt like I was stepping into the unknown, fearing how many straps I was about to endure. Brother Mahoney then whacked me again.

The pain was excruciating and took on different forms. I was clenching and releasing my hand and began walking around the room, breathing heavily, and murmuring. After I stabilised my breathing, I stepped up and raised my right hand once again. Brother Mahoney raised his arm, but as he was mid-motion, I flinched and the strap caught the tips of my fingers.

"That doesn't count," Brother Mahoney snapped. "You must not pull away, otherwise you'll have to add another strap."

I heard what was being said while I tried to deal with the pain in my fingertips by clasping and squeezing them with my left hand. I soon presented my right hand again and suffered another whack.

At this point, I yelped. My mind was in confusion, unable to comprehend what was happening to my body. I was instinctively and unthinkingly performing various actions. I clasped, rubbed, clenched, and released my hand while blowing on it to deal with an intense burning sensation. I walked around, mumbling and moaning. After I had collected myself, I looked up and saw Brother Mahoney waiting for me.

I trudged over and raised my right hand while I looked up to the heavens. All that came down was another thunderous whack.

I took leave of my senses as the pain was now unbearable. I couldn't understand how my hand could feel numb and yet be in so much pain at the same time. The pain and pulsation radiated out to my whole body. I couldn't rub, squeeze, or blow hard enough to ease the agony. When I looked at my hand, it was bright red with white streaks in places. I then glanced up and saw Brother Mahoney waiting for me. I stepped up again, raised my right hand, and, on cue, down came another tremendous whack.

"Okay, then," Brother Mahoney said in an insouciant manner. "I'll be going to see Carlo now. You can move on as soon as you pull yourself together."

Brother Mahoney collected his belongings and left. "Sorry for keeping you so long," I heard him say from the next room. "Frank held me up. As I told you before, it is unacceptable for you to treat your school uniform with disrespect." I then heard the door in the next room slam shut.

Steps sounded against timber floorboards and I knew what was coming next. I couldn't bear to hear any more, so I left. I completed my final classes before I joined Michael and Lou for the walk home.

I spent the weekend pondering what had transpired over my first week at secondary school. I'd got the strap every day in circumstances that I felt were not my fault, or where I had done nothing wrong.

My parents picked up on my pensiveness and queried my mood. I mentioned the high level of discipline at the school, without getting into details.

"Do the right thing and stay strong," my father advised. "Everything will be all right."

"It's a Catholic school with religious staff," my mother reminded me. "So, I'm sure it's for your own good."

I appreciated their well-intended sentiments and took some solace from them; nevertheless, I still feared returning to school.

# Chapter 12

## Back to School

During the following week at school, I learned that Carlo had left and enrolled in the local state school.

I recollected the advice my parents had given me and tried to hold firm and persevere.

My classes on the first few days went smoothly, without incident, which gave me some heart.

I then turned up for the Religion class taken by Brother Mahoney. He commenced a monologue covering various aspects of the Bible, during which he posed a number of ideas that fascinated me. The other students appeared uninterested until he put a question directly to us.

No one raised their hand, and Brother Mahoney asked the question again, but there was still no response. I was confident I knew the answer, but I feared putting up my hand. He became annoyed as he huffed and puffed. He then put the question to us once more, and I tentatively put up my hand.

Brother Mahoney looked towards me and raised his eyebrows. "Well then?" he said.

I gave my answer and anxiously waited for the outcome.

"Yes, that's right!" Brother Mahoney exclaimed, and completed the class with a short sermon.

The incident seemed to be the catalyst for an attitudinal change in Brother Mahoney towards me. He appeared more fair-minded, and, as a result, I became more confident in my abilities and, notwithstanding the occasional strap, I generally felt more at ease.

There were other teachers who were also liberal in handing out punitive measures. Brother Jones was in his fifties and was exceptionally resourceful in making gadgetry and being a handyman. He also ran trade workshops, such as in woodwork, which he made available to students after hours. However, his greatest satisfaction came from crafting his own straps.

Brother Jones made his straps mainly from leather, but sometimes from wood. If this wasn't strange enough, he also gave them names. His favourite straps were Woodie, being his wooden strap, and his leather straps, Brownie and Blackjack.

"Look at the fine stitching on this strap," Brother Jones would boast. "The yellow stitching really does stand out against the black leather."

Brother Jones took our Graphics classes. He would proudly stand on the platform in front of the blackboard explaining the numerous steps to create an array of lines and angles at varying degrees.

Students sat on high stools at workbenches, armed with their elaborate compass kits, paying close attention to Brother Jones's every move. However, as he exhibited the sequential steps, he would invariably move in the way.

I sat on one of the stools at a workbench in the far corner, and we had particular difficulty seeing what Brother Jones was doing.

"Excuse me, Brother," one of the students at our workbench would often say. "We can't see what you're doing as your body is in the way."

"Oh, excuse me," Brother Jones would reply, but he would soon move back in the way again. After he had completed his instructions, he would stomp down the aisle, directly to our workbench.

"Don't you know what to do? You obviously haven't been paying attention." Brother Jones accused. "Get up and raise your hand."

Brother Jones would reach for a strap that he had concealed inside his cassock. He normally had a wooden strap on one side and a leather strap on the other. He often got tangled in his clothes as he tried to extricate a strap. His standard punishment was one strap on each hand; however, as he was mildly feeble, they didn't hurt too much.

Brother Jones would then move to the next student, firing off further accusations. "You did that freehand, didn't you?"

"No, Brother, I didn't."

"Don't talk back to me. Get up and hold out your hand!"

Brother Jones then engaged in another tussle with

his garb before he managed to liberate one of his straps and dish out another dose of punishment.

The number of straps I received diminished as I got used to the school, the procedures, and the individual peculiarities of the various teachers. Nonetheless, the name-calling by the students continued, and they seemed to put more thought and creativity into the names.

I was subjected to the standard cries of Big Nose and Big Ears; however, they added Neanderthal and The Missing Link to the list. Other students were even more inventive.

"Hey Frank, you look like a yellow cab with the front doors open," one boy gleefully said.

"Hang on. Frank has one ear that sticks out more than the other," another boy pointed out as he chuckled. "So he actually looks more like a yellow cab with one front door open and the other front door only half open."

For the remainder of the year and the next couple of years, I put up with the name-calling and the occasional strap, incorporating them as part of my expected routine and accepting them as being in the nature of things.

\*　　\*　　\*

My family was working class, but Joe ensured we never went wanting. He always emphasised the highest priorities in life, being healthy food and healthy living. Ironically, the simplest things seemed to provide Jessica and me with our greatest joys.

During the cold winter months, when we had to get up early in the morning, Joe would get up earlier and light the fire. When he gave us the word, we would scurry in front of the flames, holding our clothes, so we could comfortably dress in warmth.

At the end of a cold day, Mary would place a number of hot coals into a small pot and use it as an iron to warm our sheets before we excitedly jumped into bed.

Joe put money aside for a rainy day, as well as for the occasional small indulgence. He would surprise us every so often with a little gift, such as cakes and candy.

Every Christmas, Joe would purchase a living Christmas tree from the Queen Victoria Market and, not owning a motor vehicle at the time, he would cart it home on the number 55 tram. When he arrived, Jessica and I would jump up and down with glee. It was a special event where the entire family partook in decorating the tree. The scent of pine wafting through the house added to the festive and happy mood.

Joe emphasised how critical it was to live within your means. He pointed out how he gave up drinking and smoking when his children came along. The only vice he maintained was an occasional punt on the racehorses.

In 1974, we were enjoying family lunch on the Melbourne Cup day holiday when Joe unexpectedly put a question to us. "Have we ever been to the Melbourne Cup?"

Mary, Jessica, and I looked to each other with quizzical expressions, partly due to surprise at the question and partly in reflecting on the answer.

"No, we haven't," Mary replied.

"I've never been," I said.

"Neither have I," Jessica added.

"Well, get dressed. We're going!"

There was immediate excitement as we scurried to get ready and Joe rang for a taxi, which we piled into the moment it arrived. By the time we got into Flemington Racecourse, it was 30 minutes till race time.

Joe gave Jessica and me a dollar each for a bet in the Cup. Jessica selected Big Angel to win. I couldn't pick anything, so I pocketed the dollar. Joe was keen on the favourite, Leilani.

Mary and Jessica minded our spot about 10 metres from the outside rail and 50 metres before the finishing post while Joe and I set off to place the bets.

Joe surveyed the odds, moving up and down the row of bookmakers. He appeared agitated as he turned his head one way and then the other.

"What's wrong?" I asked him.

"I was hoping to bet five dollars each way on Leilani at 4/1, but I can't seem to find anything better than 3/1 each way and 7/2 for win only. On the other hand, I can get a price of even money for place only," Joe explained. "And we don't have much time."

Joe quickly placed his bet of ten dollars on Leilani for place only and was given ten dollars change. "I gave you a fifty dollar note," Joe said. "So you need to give me another thirty dollars."

"No, sir," the bookmaker replied. "You only gave me a twenty."

"I gave you a fifty," Joe asserted.

"No, it was a twenty."

There was a large crowd, with punters pushing and buffeting to place their bets before the big race.

"I'm sure it was a fifty," Joe insisted, raising his voice.

The bookmaker maintained his composure and grudgingly handed over another thirty dollars. Joe then dashed off to another bookmaker and placed a dollar to win on Big Angel.

"Oh dear," Joe said.

"What's the matter?" I asked.

"I've got fifty dollars in my pocket and I only had one fifty-dollar bill," Joe said dispiritedly. "I made a mistake."

Joe hurriedly returned to the first bookmaker. "Excuse me, sir. I made a big mistake; you were right. I must have only handed you a twenty, as I found my fifty in another pocket," Joe explained as he returned thirty dollars.

The bookmaker snatched the thirty dollars without uttering a word. Joe and I then rushed to see the race and we got there with seconds to spare.

The horses were being loaded into the starting stalls and the intensity of the crowd was building. By the time the last horse was locked away, the crowd was bursting with anticipation. The starting gates opened and the crowd erupted with a huge roar.

The horses made their way up the straight and there was another loud roar as they went by the finishing post for the first time.

As the horses settled, High Sail was 10 lengths in the lead. Leilani settled fifth on the fence. We couldn't spot Big Angel and we didn't hear it in the call.

Jessica and I were jumping up and down in order to get a better view of the field. As the horses thundered around the home turn, the cheers and shouts from the crowd escalated to a crescendo.

Nearing the finish line, Leilani got to the lead. "Go Leilani, you beauty!" I heard my father shout. Down the outside came a horse with a blistering run. It was number 12, Think Big, which overtook the field to win.

"Bad luck," Mary told Joe.

"It's okay," Joe replied. "I backed Leilani just for the place, so I still collect."

"What about your horse?" Mary asked Jessica, but before Jessica could utter a response, we heard the race caller complete the placings. "... and the last two to come in, or last three, rather, were Passetreul, High Sail, and Big Angel almost did not complete the course."

"Never mind," Mary told Jessica.

"I'll go and collect," Joe suggested.

"I want to come too," I called out, running to catch up to him.

As we walked to the bookmaker, I looked up to my father in admiration. His honesty and high moral standards made me beam with pride. We got to the bookmaker's stand and Joe handed over the ticket to the bookie's clerk. The clerk tore the ticket and handed over twenty dollars.

"I wonder if this twenty dollars is part of the thirty dollars that I handed back?" my father quipped, and we both laughed.

# Chapter 13

## The Opposite Sex

I settled into a routine at school, although there was one main aspect of my life that seemed to be lacking, and that was interaction with the opposite sex.

In form four, when the boys were either 15 or 16 years of age, girls became more of a feature. The boys from our all-boys Catholic school would usually arrange rendezvous with girls from the local all-girls Catholic school. Some of the more brazen lads would meet up with girls from state schools, which was often the cause of interschool fights.

The usual meeting places were train stations and tram stops. The most popular girls were the stunning-lookers and the ones who put out. The most popular boys were the star athletes and good–lookers, although the sleazy bad boys also got a look in.

Naturally, given my ugly facial features and rock-bottom self-esteem, I didn't figure at all. In fact, I would tend to steer clear of the mixed-sex meetings, as the only attention I got was the usual name-calling. However, I inquisitively observed that the girls generally didn't join in with the name-calling and did not seem to get the same degree of amusement from it.

I usually walked to school, accompanied by Lou and Michael, but if they weren't around, or when the weather was inclement, I would catch public transport. One day, I was waiting for the tram when a girl named Felicity approached me.

Felicity was slim and shapely, with hazel eyes and long, blonde-brown hair featuring a front fringe. She attended the all-girls Catholic school and was unanimously considered to be the most beautiful girl of them all.

"Excuse me," I heard her say.

I didn't respond, as I assumed she was talking to someone else; however, she came closer and repeated, "Excuse me."

I looked at her, perplexed, "Are you talking to me?"

"Yeah, I was. Do you know Marcus?"

"Marcus who?"

"Marcus, the captain of your school's football team."

"I don't really know him, but I know who he is."

"Well, could you let him know that Felicity was looking for him?"

"Felicity? Does he know who you are?" I asked, even though I knew full well she was Felicity and that she was rumoured to be in a relationship with Marcus.

"Yes, I'm Felicity," she responded with a wry smile. "And I'm sure he knows who I am."

"Oh, okay. If I happen to come across Marcus, I'll let him know that Felicity, whom he should know, is looking for him," I said.

Felicity had a curious expression as she commented, "Okay. Thanks."

I never did bump into Marcus and therefore never passed on the message.

A few weeks later, I observed Felicity with a few of her girlfriends, a blush of boys surrounding them. I minded my own business, although when Felicity departed the group, she walked by me and gave me a smile. I simply observed her, expressionless.

*These girls*, I thought. *They're always playing games.*

As the year went on, the fourth-form boys were advised they would be taking ballroom dancing lessons that would culminate at the end of the year in a formal ball with the fourth-form girls at the all-girls Catholic school. The reaction from the boys was unanimous: we didn't like it at all.

Soon after, weekly dance lessons with the girls commenced. Most of the girls and boys were initially shy, although the more outgoing students were right into it. I treated the girls I encountered with respect and concentrated on the dancing. Nevertheless, I was acutely aware of the changing mood of the girls as they came into contact with me.

I couldn't help noticing how the girls generally treated the uglier and more subdued boys with formality, impassiveness, and demureness. On the other hand, they treated the handsome and entertaining boys with effervescence, forwardness, and sensuality.

The exception to this general rule was Felicity; not only was she beautiful, but she also appeared to be genuinely friendly with everyone she met.

I came alive whenever we changed partners and I found her in my arms. I was bedazzled by her looks, despite the fact I couldn't help seeing my grotesque features mirrored in her alluring eyes. However, she was quick to put me at ease and it was mainly through her that I discovered I had a good sense of humour and a clever wit.

"You look off-colour today," Felicity told me.

"I'm really a night person," I replied.

"Why? What do you get up to?"

"Sleep," I said with a grin, and she laughed.

We smiled at each other as she progressed to the next dancer and I felt her fingertips slip out of my hand. I was greeted by my new partner, who gave me a 'dead fish' handshake.

Towards the end of the year, the formal dance came around. I was not looking forward to the event, particularly as a number of the boys and girls were going steady or were paired off.

Mary and Jessica were much more delighted about the formal than I was. They assisted me with my suit, and Joe did up my bow tie.

"You know, when I went to dances in my younger days, I would start with the prettiest girls and ask each one to dance until I got a 'yes', even if it was the last girl in the place," Joe explained. "Do you know what I'm saying?"

"Yes, I think so," I replied. "I should never be put off by rejection."

"That's right."

I knew my dad meant well, but I also knew he was exceptionally handsome in his younger days, very sociable, with a lively personality. I also suspected not many women would have rejected him. Nevertheless, I appreciated his sentiments.

We heard the bell ring, and Jessica rushed to open the front door. "Michael and Lou are here," she shouted excitedly.

The three of us checked each other out, and there were compliments all round, although I knew Michael and Lou, unlike myself, really did look good.

Michael was tall and slim, with light-brown hair and hazel eyes. Lou was of average height, with blond hair and deep-blue eyes. They were both exceptionally good-looking and, obviously, extremely popular with the girls.

We headed off, with Michael's father driving us to the venue. As soon as we arrived and walked into the reception hall, both Michael and Lou were swamped by a bevy of girls and they eagerly filled out their dance cards.

I walked along the side wall and met up with some of the shyer boys I knew. We observed the activities around the hall, paying particular attention to the apparently available girls.

The headmaster made some welcoming comments and wished everyone an enjoyable evening. The Master of Ceremonies lightened the mood and introduced the first dance.

Felicity approached me. "Hello Frank."

"Hi Felicity. How are you?"

"I'm really good. I was wondering whether you had an empty space on your dance card to fit me in."

"Yeah, I have an empty space."

"Well, I've got one spare space, but it happens to be the last dance."

"The last dance," I repeated, finding it incredulous that she hadn't filled in her last dance. "Are you sure there isn't anyone else you want to choose for the last dance?"

"No," she said. "In fact, I kept the last dance for you."

"Okay," I said, hesitatingly. "I'd be honoured to dance with you."

"Fantastic!" Felicity exclaimed as the music commenced and she skipped away.

Partners lined up and commenced dancing. My head was in a spin as I tried to rationalise the situation. *Why would she want to have the last dance with me? Why would she want to dance with me at all?*

I was walking around the hall, crunching my dance card in my hand. As one dance progressed to the next, I got more nervous. I was then inundated with overwhelming thoughts.

*Why am I still clutching my dance card? I'm not going to*

have any more dances now. I've only got the one dance, and it's the last dance, so it shouldn't be too hard to work out.

I tried to figure out why Felicity would ask to have the last dance with me and a number of malevolent thoughts pervaded my mind.

*Is this part of some sick joke? Felicity is such a genuinely lovely person; however, what if it's all been just an act. Maybe she's trying to make someone else jealous. That's it! She's just using me, being an ugly guy, to make a boy she's keen on jealous. That's okay; I can accept that.*

I felt more at ease as an intermission was announced. As the dancing was about to recommence, Felicity passed by. "I hope you haven't forgotten our dance," she said.

"What dance?" I quipped. "Only joking. Of course I remember."

I continued walking around the hall and, for some inexplicable reason, I started to fret again and began to get cold feet. I was feeling nauseated, so I rushed to the toilet, where I entered a cubicle and locked the door. I pulled down my pants, took a seat, and placed my head in my hands. I then experienced an overwhelming urge to cry. After a few moments, my responsibility to honour my promise forced me to step out for the last dance.

I re-entered the hall and the music started playing. I glanced around and noticed Felicity on her own in the middle of the dance floor.

"What dance is this?" I asked the people closest to me.

"It's the last dance."

I rushed over and stopped in front of Felicity.

"I thought you had forgotten our dance after all," she said with a smile.

"No," I replied. "I'm just fashionably late. I'm sorry."

Felicity grinned. We simultaneously assumed the waltz closed position, counted to the music, and commenced dancing. We were silent for a few moments as we got into the groove.

"You're a very good dancer," Felicity said.

"I should be, as I practice a lot."

"Who's the lucky girl who practices with you?"

"My blow-up doll."

Felicity looked startled, and I smiled. "You're hopeless," she said.

"Do you know how to give a blow-up doll a sex change?"

"No, I don't, and I'm not sure I want to know, but go on."

"You turn them inside out."

Felicity gave me a playful slap on the shoulder as she rolled her eyes and eventually broke into a laugh. We didn't utter another word. I fell into an ethereal state until the music stopped and we stood still, facing each other.

"Thank you for the dance, Felicity. It was the highlight of my night."

"It was my pleasure, Frank. I enjoyed it too."

I was looking into Felicity's beautiful eyes when I

noticed a number of boys encroaching upon us.

"Well, I'd better get going as I've got a lift home," I said.

"Oh, okay. I hope to see you around."

"Yeah, sure," I said, as I let go of her hand and wandered off to locate Michael and Lou. I looked back to see Felicity swarmed by boys.

Lou and Michael were in close proximity, bidding farewell to their respective sweethearts. They eventually extricated themselves and we walked out.

"How was your night?" Michael asked me on the way to his father's car.

"It was good," I replied with a rueful smile.

# Chapter 14

## Our School Excursion

Another feature of the year for fourth-form students was the opportunity to go on a two-night expedition to a Victorian farm. The trip promised a time for learning, adventure, and fun. However, the expedition was optional and had to be funded by parents.

Information promoting the trip was handed out to students to take home and they had a week to provide their responses. If students wished to attend, they were required to provide the cash payment.

I perused the promotional material and it piqued my interest; however, I was aware that it wasn't cheap, so I tempered my enthusiasm.

When I arrived home, I went about my usual routine and acted as normal as I could. While Mary prepared dinner, I gave her a hand. Jessica was reading in her room and Joe was dealing with some administrative matters at his writing desk. At precisely six o'clock, Joe yelled out, "It's time for the news," which attracted us to the lounge.

Mary alternated between the kitchen and the lounge, to ensure dinner was on track. At the end of the news, at half past six, we all adjourned to the kitchen. There wasn't much discussion over dinner, with the major topic being comments and compliments regarding the meal.

After dinner, Jessica gave Mary a hand with the washing up and drying, while Joe and I played a few hands of cards. During the game, Joe asked how things were at school. I mentioned the excursion and he asked to see the information.

Joe strolled into the lounge, perusing the material, and took a seat on his beloved recliner. I followed him, turned on the television, and sat on the couch. I feigned watching the television when I was actually focussed on Joe. When he finished reading, he tossed the material on the coffee table and looked towards the television.

I interpreted Joe's action to be dismissive of the trip and resigned myself to the fact that he wouldn't consider it. However, when the commercials came on, he turned to me. "Did you want to go on this trip?"

"I'm not fussed either way," I replied.

"Are your friends going?"

"Lou and Michael both said they would probably go, but their parents are rich."

The television program came back on and Joe was silent until the commercials featured again. "When do you need to decide and pay?"

"By the end of next week."

The program came back on and no further word was spoken about the matter for the rest of the weekend.

I returned to school on Monday and there was raised excitement as the students discussed the prospect of the excursion.

Joe was silent on the matter until Wednesday evening. "Did you want to go on that trip?" he asked again.

"I wouldn't mind," I said. "But it's very expensive and probably not worth the money."

"I think you should go," said Joe.

"But what about the money?" I asked.

"We can manage it," Joe assured me. "In fact, I've got the money right here."

I knew that this gesture by my parents was a significant sacrifice. "Thank you, Dad," I said as I walked across and hugged him. Mary overheard my happy sentiments and appeared in the doorway wearing a beaming smile. As soon as I saw her, I ran over and hugged her too. "Thank you, Mum."

I was ecstatic that I was able to attend the excursion, particularly as all the other students in my class were going, with a couple of the poorer families being provided financial assistance.

The participating students received a list of items recommended for the trip. There was excited discussion on a daily basis as we ticked off the items. In the days ahead of the excursion, the students were gripped with heightened anticipation.

On the evening before departure, my parents helped me pack. I could not contain my happiness, especially since my mother looked joyous and my father contented.

It was an early-morning start, with Lou and I separately making our way to Michael's place, from whence his father drove us to school. We then boarded a bus for the six-hour ride to the farm. We were allowed to find our own seats. The unruly boys muscled their way to the back, while Michael, Lou, Reno, and I took seats halfway down the bus, with Michael sitting next to Lou and Reno next to me.

Brother Mahoney and Brother Smith accompanied us. Brother Smith sat in the front seat across from the driver. The two seats behind the driver were vacant, and Brother Mahoney assumed one of those.

We spent the time singing songs, including the school song, enjoying the views, and mucking about. It was about three hours into the ride when we stopped for lunch.

After we resumed, it wasn't long before Brother Mahoney got up from his seat, with Brother Smith looking over his shoulder and giving Brother Mahoney a creepy smile.

Brother Smith's reaction sent shivers down my spine — a sensation I had not previously felt — and caused me to pay acute attention to what was going on.

Brother Mahoney walked up and down the aisle with his usual stunned expression. There were several boys who were enjoying two seats to themselves, and Brother Mahoney examined each of them before he selected one to sit next to, which was a couple of seats ahead of me on the other side of the bus.

I continued observing with curiosity when I saw Brother Mahoney place his arm around the boy's shoulders. As soon as this occurred, I nudged Reno and nodded in their direction. Reno looked over and, after a few moments, turned to me with an expression that matched my feeling of concern.

Soon after, Brother Mahoney took his other arm off the arm rest and moved it out of our sight. Reno and I looked at each other with dismay. I then nudged Michael in front of me and pointed in that direction. It wasn't long before he was nudging Lou and they were looking back at Reno and I, shrugging their shoulders, confused.

None of us knew what was going on, but all four of us felt uncomfortable. Brother Mahoney must have sat there for almost half an hour before he resumed his original seat.

After a while, Brother Mahoney was up again, sitting next to another boy directly ahead of us. Even though they were out of our sight, the four of us gasped with despair.

The bus ride eventually came to an end, to the excitement of most students, although Michael, Lou, Reno, and I sighed with relief. We looked at the boys with whom Brother Mahoney had sat, but they did not manifest any signs of harm or distress, so we assumed we had misconstrued events.

We trekked to the farmhouse, which consisted of

numerous rooms with bunk beds, with four beds per room. To my disappointment, the beds were allocated and I was made to bunk with three boys I didn't know very well, two of whom I did not like.

We had time to settle in before we were shown around the farm and met the resident cows, horses, chickens, and pigs. A bell sounded, which was the call for dinner. I was pleased to be seated with my friends and enjoyed a hearty meal of assorted meats, vegetables, and salads. During dinner, we were invited to go spotlighting. I had no idea what it was, but I assumed it involved spotting bush animals.

We grabbed our winter coats and ran out the farmhouse to where five open-tray, off-road vehicles stood. Each vehicle had two large spotlights in front and a mounted spotlight on the back, operated by a farmhand. Each driver had a dog in their passenger seat. The students jumped on the back of the vehicles, and I found one of the remaining positions.

We sped off and the students hung on for dear life as they shouted and cheered. The vehicles were sliding all over the dirt tracks, which had turned to mud given the wet weather of recent days.

We proceeded in different directions and the ride got a lot bumpier. It was exhilarating, though, and even I got caught up in the excitement.

"There are some over there!" shouted the farmhand as he pointed. The driver slowly drove in that direction and the spotlight picked up a couple of rabbits scurrying through the brush.

The farmhand spotted a rabbit and shone the spotlight straight into its eyes. The driver slowly stopped the vehicle and opened the passenger door to let the dog out, as he jumped out the driver's door.

Everything happened so quickly as the dog cunningly approached the rabbit and the driver captured it. The farmhand jumped off the back and we followed him. The driver held the rabbit by the back legs, allowing it to hang. The farmhand had a heavy stick and he whacked the rabbit behind the ears. The animal wriggled for a few seconds and was then motionless.

"That's how you do it," the driver instructed. "One swift hit on the back of the head, just behind the ears, and it's dead."

"What about that wiggling?" I asked.

"That's just nerves," the farmhand curtly replied.

We reboarded the vehicle and repeated the same process over and over with each student having a go at killing the rabbit, with different levels of success, which meant some of the creatures had to endure varying degrees of torture.

The driver indicated we had to get back soon and he set off for a final foray. They tracked another rabbit and were soon mesmerising it with the spotlight. I followed the group, although I stood back and was looking away.

"Has everyone had a go?" the driver asked.

I heard the students take their turn to confirm they had. "I think we all have," the last student in the group said, but then he turned and noticed me. "Hang on. I don't think Frank has had a turn."

I turned to look at them. "That's okay," I said. "I'm not fussed."

"Come on, Frank," another boy said.

"Yeah, come on," yet another boy insisted. "We've all had a go, so why don't you have a go too?"

By this time, there was shouting and screaming as the boys egged me on. I looked at the helpless rabbit hanging upside down, appearing petrified.

*I have to put this poor creature out of its misery,* logic told me and, without any further thought, I stepped forward, grabbed the stick out of a boy's hand, and gave the rabbit an almighty whack on the back of its head. The rabbit almost shot out of the driver's hand as it immediately fell limp without any wiggling.

The students congratulated me for the strike and there was much euphoria as we completed the hunt. When we returned to the farmhouse there was a great deal of chatter about the adventure, while I was depressed and shocked.

We eventually retired to our bunks. I was the last to enter the bedroom and noticed that John was already in a bottom bunk. John was a short, quiet student who generally kept to himself.

I then saw Phil in the bunk above him. As soon as he sensed my arrival, he turned towards me, raised himself on his elbow, and eyed me without uttering a word. Phil was of average height and build and was known as a bit of a trouble-maker and a practical-joker. I hated practical-jokers.

The other bottom bunk had a backpack on it, and I heard water running in the bathroom, so I assumed it was Garry's.

Garry was tall and thin, but he had tremendous physical strength and was renowned for his tough-guy reputation — one of the few boys I really feared. I opened my backpack, pulled out my toiletries, and waited for my turn in the bathroom.

"Well, look who we've got here," Garry commented as he entered the room.

I didn't respond as I made my way into the bathroom, taking my toiletries and pyjamas with me. When I returned, the lights had been turned off. As the light switch was reachable from my bunk, I switched on the lights.

"What the hell are you doing?" Garry asked aggressively.

I considered that it was obvious what I was doing, so I didn't respond. I simply went about my business, getting in the top bunk above Garry and switching off the light.

"You'd better watch out, Frank," Garry said in a threatening voice. "When you least expect it, expect it, as something really bad might happen to you."

I was alarmed, as Garry was not one to make idle threats. However, my mind was recalling the poor rabbits.

"Yep, when you least expect it, you're going to be taught a serious lesson," Garry said, and continued his warnings as he started shaking the bunk.

I was confused, my fear of Garry enmeshed with what I'd witnessed with the rabbits. I was having mixed emotions of fear, depression, and frustration. As Garry continued shaking the bed and mouthing off, my nerves got the better of me and I involuntarily uttered in a firm, loud voice, "Fuck off, Garry!"

The moment I made the statement I was stunned. I couldn't believe I'd actually said it. If I could have taken it back, I would have done so in a heartbeat. I was terrified as I waited for a response, but there wasn't one. I stayed wide awake, clutching the blankets under my chin most of the night, waiting for Garry to act. However, there was only an eerie silence. It was solely due to exhaustion that I managed to get some sleep.

A rooster was the early-morning wakeup call. I waited for the others to get up and get changed before I made a move. By this time, the brothers and farmhands were coming around to hurry the stragglers.

We were taken in turns to witness the cows being milked before we had breakfast. We were then given a tour of the surrounding agricultural fields and storage facilities.

After lunch, we wandered outside to where a dozen horses stood saddled. I happened to be the first in line and I was handed the reins to a striking black horse. The other students were envious of me as they were handed the reins to their horses.

"Why does he get the black horse?" the other boys complained. However, the complaints were ignored as we were shown how to mount and the farmhands went around giving everyone a leg up.

My horse was beautiful and docile. I had never ridden a horse before and had no idea what to do. I tried to follow the riding instructions we were given, to limited success. Fortunately, the horses knew the path and did their own thing.

The farmhands were highly experienced and extremely helpful. It was halfway into the ride when one of them asked if I wanted my horse to run. I declined, but my answer was completely disregarded as, the next thing I knew, I was hanging on for dear life.

My horse slowed of its own accord and passively led me back. I was invigorated by the ride and, as I approached the farmhouse, a number of boys rushed towards me to have their turn, and they all wanted my horse.

I felt my horse buck and shy away as it took fright. I also took fright as I became airborne, and my unexpected freefall caused me to gasp for air. There were shrieks of concern, but I also heard the distinct sound of laughter. Fortunately, I came down on thick grass and was unscathed. I looked up to see that the laughter emanated from Garry.

After dinner, we migrated to a large living room featuring a huge fireplace. Everyone found a seat, whether it be on the couch or on the rug, encircling the fireplace. Brother Smith plonked himself on one of the armchairs and Brother Mahoney on the other. There was lively discussion about the events of the day, which tired everyone and prepared us for slumber.

John and I were quick to be the first to bed, while Garry entered with Phil and they slowly hit the sack. When Garry got into his bunk, I heard him whisper, "When you least expect it."

The next day was cold and wet, so we spent it in the farmhouse. We alternated doing various activities such as reading, darts, Kelly pool, table tennis, and playing cards.

After lunch, I went to the bedroom to collect a pullover. I was rummaging through my backpack when I heard the door bang shut. I whirled to witness Garry hurl himself upon me.

Garry was vicious in his attack as he got hold of my collar and held me down with one arm, preparing to clobber me with the other. I fell back, over my backpack, and tried to scurry away. He grabbed me by the ankles as I attempted to rise and I stumbled on my back onto his bunk. He then leaped onto the bunk after me.

Somehow, I managed to bring my knees to my chest, my feet on his chest, and I had both hands clasping his heavy, woollen pullover. I then screamed out, "Stop!"

Garry gave me a menacing stare, but he did momentarily halt.

"I don't want any trouble, but if you don't leave me alone I am going to hurt you by banging your head against the wooden beam just above you."

Garry rolled his eyes up, but he couldn't see the beam above him. He seemed to be thinking over the matter and I felt that I had to make a move. I kicked up with all my might and heard his head bang against the beam. He seemed stunned, although I could still feel his strength bearing down on me.

"That was just a love tap," I told him. "You've got one last chance to tell me you'll leave me alone."

"Okay," he said to my astonishment and he eased back.

I stayed in my position until I saw Garry leave the room. I then got up and peeked out the door. He was gingerly walking down the hall and I surmised I'd injured him more than I thought and a lot more than I had intended. To my amazement, he never gave me any trouble from that day on.

Dinner time was soon upon us and we were promised a special treat. I was keen to know what it was, until I learned it was stewed rabbit. Yes, they were the very rabbits we had caught the previous day.

I didn't have too much of an appetite and settled on everything bar the rabbit. Even so, I could not avoid the aroma, the incessant descriptions of the taste, and compliments towards the cooks, who gave a detailed description of the cooking process.

Early morning, we packed for the ride home. However, rather than taking a bus, we were going back by train. We were shuttled to the station and boarded. I sat in a booth with Reno, Michael, and Lou, comfortable that the brothers were not in our cabin. To our disappointment, Brother Mahoney soon made an appearance and took a seat next to one of the other boys.

"Oh, it's so cold," Brother Mahoney commented as he unashamedly cuddled up to the boy next to him and placed his hands inside the boy's pullover.

We looked at one another with consternation before the four of us peered out the window. Even though I was facing a picturesque landscape, I didn't take in any of the scenery, as my mind was in a spin and I didn't know what to think.

# Chapter 15

## Church Child Abuse

The strange incidences concerning Brother Mahoney caused me to cast my mind back to past affairs, which I hadn't thought much of at the time, as well as becoming more attuned to future events.

One of our parish priests was Father Nero. He was a jolly and lively priest who was widely believed to have a drinking problem. He celebrated numerous masses every week and parishioners could evidence him liberally partaking in the libations.

Every time I attended a mass that Father Nero conducted, he would spend an inordinate amount of time celebrating the Eucharist. He would serve Holy Communion, then return to the communion table and indulge in gulps of the sacramental wine. After consuming the chalice, he would pour more wine from the cruet into the chalice and drink the entire contents once more.

Father Nero often organised fetes and outings. In preparation for the events, he would select a number of helpers, mainly young boys, who could be seen going in and out of the presbytery at all hours.

Father Nero left the parish under mysterious

circumstances. Some people suspected it was due to his drinking. Others suggested he was misappropriating money from his organised events. However, there was a lingering rumour that there was a much more serious and sinister reason.

*   *   *

Returning to secondary school after the farm excursion, Brother Mahoney's actions became more conspicuous. He sometimes arranged working bees with students that were run over the weekends.

On one occasion, Lou hadn't completed one of his assignments by the Friday deadline and Brother Mahoney allowed him to hand it in on Saturday morning. Michael didn't attend school that day, and Lou sought me out to walk home with him.

"Brother Mahoney wants me to hand in an assignment tomorrow morning," Lou divulged.

When I looked over at Lou, he appeared worried, and I could appreciate why. "I'm happy to go with you," I suggested.

"You don't mind?" Lou asked, perking up.

"No, I don't mind at all," I responded with a grin.

On Saturday morning, Lou passed by my house and we walked to school. The school was closed, but we heard noises in the adjacent monastery. Lou walked towards the front door, which stood open, although the front screen door was closed. Lou was about to ring the bell when a boy exited the monastery and walked off. Lou and I looked at each other with concern, but we didn't make a move.

After a little while, Brother Mahoney emerged. "Oh, hello Lou. It slipped my mind that you were coming," he said as he approached. He then noticed me and gave me a glaring stare.

Brother Mahoney was wearing black pants, a black shirt that had the top three buttons undone, and black shoes. He was unshaven, had dishevelled hair, and stunk to high heaven of smoke, alcohol, and who knew what else.

"This must be your assignment," Brother Mahoney said. Lou nodded and handed it over. "You can run along now."

Lou and I couldn't get out of there fast enough.

Our Religion classes went from the unusual to the bizarre. Brother Mahoney commenced in the classroom, progressed outdoors on fine days, and sometimes we ended up in one of the large rooms in the monastery.

On one occasion, Brother Mahoney directed the Religion class students into the living room of the monastery. He instructed us to find a place on the carpeted floor and lie down. He then closed the blinds, which darkened the room, and told us to close our eyes and relax.

Brother Mahoney put on recorded noises of nature, such as running water, rustling leaves, and whistling wind. As I listened, I thought I sensed some movement in the room. I tried to concentrate on the movement sounds, but I lost them. We had to endure the nature noises for a while and then I thought I heard movement again, but only for a few moments. Soon after, Brother Mahoney opened the blinds and turned off the sound recording.

Our eyes had to adjust to the sunlight. I looked around the room to see students blinking or rubbing their eyes, as if they had come out of a deep sleep. Although I felt something strange had gone on, I couldn't evidence anything untoward.

I was glad to complete form four, which meant it was time for students to progress to another secondary school, as ours only taught forms one to four. I was happy to learn Michael was going to the same school I was. However, we were disappointed that Lou was heading to a coeducational college.

It was years later when we learned of the numerous charges of child abuse against certain clergy from our church and former schools.

# Chapter 16

## My First Time

On the morning of my first day at my new secondary school, Joe woke me and tried to get me up a number of times before I dragged myself out of bed. I was expecting Michael to pass by, so when I heard the doorbell ring, I quickly finished breakfast and collected my belongings. Mary and Joe kissed me goodbye and wished me good luck as I exited the house.

Walking to the tram stop, Michael and I allowed a number of trams that were jam-packed with passengers to pass by. The tram line was mainly frequented by girls and boys from the Catholic schools in North Melbourne. We eventually caught a tram and took the journey standing up.

Michael and I were the last two students to arrive, and we located our classrooms. I was disappointed to learn we were in different fifth-form classes, so I left him and made my way to room four.

I was taken aback by the appearance of the other students. Whereas the majority of the students at my previous secondary school were from Italian backgrounds, the students at this school appeared to be Anglo-Saxon and from more well-to-do families.

A boy from my previous school, named Enzo, recognised me and approached. He made me feel more at ease and I was happy to share a two-seater desk with him. We had similar feelings of ostracisation from the rest of the class. In fact, for me, it was a culture shock.

I had enormous difficulty making new friends at the new school, as did Enzo and Michael, so we tended to stick together.

I was still being called names, although the abuse took on a more strategic and psychological form. Several students talked about me in my presence by referencing people with abnormalities and disabilities.

On one occasion, a student broke away from the group and approached me. "Hey Frank, I think I know why one of your ears sticks out more than the other," he said with a grin. "When you were born, the doctor pulled you out by one ear. He took one look at your ugly face and then pushed you back in by the other ear."

I returned a wry smile and didn't say a word; however, the other students were falling over with laughter.

I was alone when I caught the tram home that day. There were a number of spare seats and I took one across the way from an elderly man. I could see out of the corner of my eye that the man kept staring at me, but I ignored him. After a few minutes, the old man got up, walked across, and sat down opposite me. I still ignored him as I continued to look out the window.

"Do you know what ANZAC stands for?" he asked me. I turned to him and was about to answer when he interrupted me. "You wouldn't know cos you're a bloody wog! Why don't you go back to your own country, you wog?"

I was stunned by the comment. I stood up, walked to the doorway, and pulled the chord, sensing the man's eyes follow me. I got off at the next stop, which was well before where I normally got off. As I walked home, tears filled my eyes and numerous thoughts entered my mind. *If it's not my physical appearance, it's my ethnic background. Will the abuse never end?*

I subsequently thought back to what the old man had said and wondered why I cried after he called me a wog. I had been called 'wog' numerous times before and, even though it hurt me, it had never driven me to tears.

I considered whether I'd cried because the old man had also commented about going back to my own country. I never considered myself to be a true-blue, dinky-di Australian like the Anglo-Saxon Australians; however, I didn't know that I could belong to another country. I racked my brain over this possibility for a number of years, until my parents visited the Italian consulate one day and I asked the consular officer whether I'd be eligible for an Italian passport.

"Unfortunately, unlike your sister, both of your parents were naturalised Australian citizens when you were born," he said. "Therefore, the Italian government does not recognise you."

I took the news rather hard, as I concluded that I was a person without a country, a stateless person, a persona non grata. Even though my assessment was not technically correct, it reflected the way I felt and I accepted it as a fact.

*     *     *

I was grateful to have friends like Enzo and Michael. I felt I could rely on them and I started to spend most of my schooldays with them. The direct result of this was that I became involved in high jinks and neglected my school work.

Over the weekends, Michael and I would often reunite with Lou. They were popular with the girls and invariably hooked up with many of them. They invited me to most of their social events, introduced me to numerous girls, and engaged me in their conversations. I really appreciated them as being the best friends a guy could have and I felt enormously indebted to them. Even though I would end up on my own, I thoroughly enjoyed the festivities and to be in the girls' presence.

Lou had befriended a number of girls from his coeducational school and we would attend numerous parties together. On one occasion, he invited me to a house party. As Michael wasn't available to go, I made the short walk to Lou's place. I was greeted by Lou and a couple of his friends from the gym. Lou's friends were a year or two older than us and one of them drove us to the party.

The house was a grungy, run-down, brick veneer in the outer northern suburbs of Melbourne. The front door was open, so we just walked in. As we proceeded down the central corridor I peeked in the open doors. There were several girls and a few guys inside the house who were smoking and drinking all sorts of substances.

Lou and one of his gym friends sat on a couch and Lou patted the spare seat for me join them. As soon as I relaxed in my seat, I was handed a can of beer. I took out my packet of cigarettes and offered them around.

We were comfortably seated and engaging in small talk. "I've often said that Frank should come down to the gym," Lou told his friend. "He works out at home and has built up his body a little, but he could do so much better with the facilities at the gym."

"I'm happy just mucking about at home," I said. "I'm not really interested in going to a gym."

"You should just come down for a look," Lou's friend suggested. "Lou's an absolute dynamo in the gym and he's training for the junior bodybuilding championships."

"That's great, Lou," I remarked. "I personally wouldn't like the idea of having people look at me."

As we were talking, a couple of new girls entered the house. One of them recognised Lou, jumped on top of him, and they started pashing. Lou's friend was soon off to talk to a couple of girls and I was left gazing about the room.

I noticed a spare couch chair and moseyed over to sit on it. I looked about the room as I smoked and drank. I then took a closer look at the other new girl. She had bleached-blonde hair and gothic make-up — dark-coloured eye liner, dark lipstick, and pale skin. She was wearing tight blue jeans and a woollen white pullover. Her eyes were slowly wandering and I looked away as they were about to meet up with mine.

I was staring at the ceiling when a shadow appeared. I looked up to find the goth girl standing over me. As I gazed at her, she held out her hand. I glanced left and right to witness that everyone else was doing their own thing, oblivious to us. I took her hand and she led me to the middle of the room.

Psychedelic music was softly playing. She placed her arms around my neck and started swaying to the music. I reacted by placing my arms around her waist and following her movements. As we slow-danced, my mind wandered. *She must be older than me. I'm 16, so I guess she's 17, or maybe 18.*

I could feel the shape of her body: her firm, rounded buttocks, her slim waist, and her taut, pointed breasts. As I grew more conscious of her external sex anatomy, I became stimulated and my

106

penis stiffened. I was embarrassed and tried to draw my groin away from her, but she pulled me closer.

When the song finished, she stopped dancing and led me along the corridor, into a vacant room. She closed the door behind us, guided me to the edge of the bed, and pushed me onto it. I obediently reclined and followed her every move. She looked down on me and her eyes did not leave mine.

As I inspected her more closely, I was struck by her beautiful features. She had alluring, large brown eyes, a cute, turned-up nose, and full, seductive lips.

She pulled her jumper over her head and threw it on a chair. She slowly unbuttoned her shirt to reveal her glorious, rounded breasts with erect nipples. She then removed her jeans and panties. Without hesitation, she bent over me, unzipped my pants, and pulled them with my jocks down to my knees. She undid the buttons of my shirt and caressed my stomach and chest. She slid down my body and I felt her tongue licking my testicles before she took my cock in her mouth.

I couldn't believe what was happening, although the heightened sensations I enjoyed from the sucking of her warm, wet mouth made it all too real.

She then mounted me and guided my cock into her. She routinely gyrated, rotated, and moved up and down as she fondled her breasts. I was just lying back, enjoying the moment, not moving, not thinking of moving in case I disturbed the experience.

She then took my hands and placed them on her

breasts. I didn't even have to think about it as I instinctively cupped them and softly pinched her nipples.

She lowered herself until our lips met and we began to kiss passionately. She forced her tongue down my throat and I instinctively sucked on it. I reached orgasm inside her, which she seemed to sense as she calmly hopped off me.

I did not move as I observed her take some tissues, wipe herself dry, and get dressed. When she left the room, I momentarily stayed on the bed to reflect. It was my first time and I was no longer a virgin. Who would have thought?

By the time I departed the room, she was nowhere to be seen. I resumed my seat on the couch until Lou made an appearance. "We can leave as soon as my friend gets back, which shouldn't take too long," he advised.

As we waited, I couldn't help thinking about the goth girl and my agitation grew to the point where I had to ask Lou about her. "Do you know the girl who was with your friend?"

"No, I've never seen her before, and my girlfriend doesn't know her either," Lou informed me. "I saw you with her. So what's her name?"

"I don't know," I replied and then pondered on the fact that neither the girl nor I had uttered a single word.

# Chapter 17

## Going Off Track

Michael and I habitually went to school together. He would come by my house and, notwithstanding my father urging and berating me to get up, I was invariably late.

Michael and I would often allow the packed trams to roll by before we got on board. At times, rather than waiting at the tram stop, we would start walking towards the school, sometimes even walking the five kilometres all the way there. Needless to say, we were always late.

We both struggled to fit in at the new school. He lost interest in his studies and was consistently getting poor grades.

Whereas in the past I had used the pursuit of my studies and the faith in my religion as a refuge, my interest in both now started to wane. Instead, I allowed the continual name-calling to get to me and I was letting out my frustrations by missing classes, mucking about, neglecting my studies, working out at my home gym, smoking, drinking, and sneaking out at night.

Lou and I would go out on Friday and Saturday

nights. Even though we were under age, we would buy alcohol and cigarettes and consume them in the streets. We would then hit the pubs and clubs. Sometimes we were allowed in and sometimes we weren't. Either way, we always caused some trouble.

Lou enjoyed picking fights with the bouncers inside or outside the clubs. He was banned from the Bombay Rock club and often had run-ins with the cops.

On one occasion when the police stopped us in the street, they asked us our names and what we were up to.

"I'm Frank Capri, and we're just on our way home," I replied.

"What about you?" the policeman asked Lou. "What's your name?"

"Tony McGregor," Lou replied.

I looked at Lou, stunned.

"How do you spell that?" the policeman asked.

Lou's eyes widened as he turned his mind to how it could possibly be spelt.

"I assume it's Mc rather than Mac?" the policeman eventually added.

Lou appeared slightly relieved as he responded, "Yeah, that's right."

After taking down the names, the policemen headed off.

"Why did you give them a false name?" I asked Lou.

"So they won't be able to locate me, of course."

"But I gave them my real name."

"Well, that's your problem."

"You don't think they'll locate you through me?" I asked Lou.

"That's right, you can't lie, can you? You bastard."

*     *     *

Even though I had gone rogue in my living habits, I still managed to hold my grades during form five; however, when I reached form six, they took a dive. Whereas before I was getting A's and B's, my grades were now D's and E's.

I was not overly upset about the situation, as I had half expected it, although I had not anticipated how hard my parents would take it.

"You're not stupid, because when they tested your IQ at school they said you were above average. In fact, I believe you were rated superior. So how could you do this to us?" Joe asked as Mary looked on, caringly but serious.

"I didn't do this to you," I replied. "I would never do this to you. I did it to myself."

"You are us! You are a product of us. Your mother never had the opportunity to go to school past primary school. She was only 12 when she had to get up at four o'clock in the morning to work on the family farm."

As my father spoke, I felt like my heart was being wrenched from my body. I was embarrassed and ashamed.

"We work hard to give you every opportunity, and what do you do?" Joe continued. "You waste your time and our money, but worst of all, you disappoint your family."

Tears were welling in my eyes and I lowered my head.

Joe steeled himself as he placed a hand firmly on my shoulder and strengthened his tone. "The Higher School Certificate is the most important year in your education, as it opens up opportunities for the rest of your life. I hope you can turn things around and make us proud."

I looked up to see my mother with her head bowed and my father looking imploringly at me. I then got up and headed to my room.

"Where are you going?" Mary asked me with tear-filled eyes.

"I'm going to my room to study."

I only had the final trimester to turn things around. I went with Michael to school on time, I paid acute attention in class, and I spent all my spare time on my homework.

The time for the final examinations was soon upon me. My parents wished me luck, with Mary giving me a kiss on each cheek. Jessica, who had starred in her sixth-form exams and received a scholarship and studentship to the University of Melbourne, stirred me on. "You can do this."

As I made my way to my first exam, I had serious

doubts. I had tried to cram a year of study into a few months and I was grossly underprepared. Nevertheless, I soldiered on, even though I felt like I was walking to my doom.

When I completed my final examination, I was relieved to have finished, but I wasn't at all confident, as I knew I had performed below my best. Nevertheless, I crossed my fingers and held out hope.

There was great anticipation as the examination results were mailed out. I stayed in my room when the results were due and did not check the mail box. On the other hand, Joe would wait each day at the front gate, looking up the street for the postman, as Mary gazed out the front room window.

I heard a knock on my bedroom door. My parents slowly entered and sat on the edge of my bed. Joe had a letter in his hand and he offered it to me. I looked to him and his eyes lit up with eager anticipation. I took the letter and held it in my hand.

I found a gap in the corner of the envelope and tore it open. I looked the document over — the front, the back, and then the front again — but I didn't make any comment. My parents looked on earnestly, in silence.

My father could no longer wait. "Did you pass?"

"The Victorian Universities and Schools Examination Board states that I have satisfied the university entrance requirements," I read out. "So I guess I passed."

I heard my mother sigh with relief as she hugged

113

me. "Thank God!" she declared.

My father smiled as he shook my hand. "Congratulations, son!"

I was still trying to read the results as my parents celebrated. I wasn't sure whether I should be happy or not as, although I had passed all of my subjects, I had only received a C average. I then did the sums in my head, based on the standardised scores, and worked out I had an Anderson score of over 250, which was the entry requirement of the university course I was seeking.

*I guess I should be happy*, I thought and then reconsidered the matter. *In fact, I've made my parents happy, so I most definitely should be happy.* I then joined in the celebrations.

# Chapter 18

## A Bent Religion

During my fifth-form and sixth-form years, when I had become more rebellious, I had also become more cynical, and I targeted my aggression towards the organisation I considered the most egregious — the Roman Catholic Church.

I began to question the brothers and priests in class when I considered the statements they made to be dubious, unfounded, or irrational. I was annoyed when I thought the responses they gave were unsatisfactory or irrelevant; however, I felt positively insulted when they appeared ignorant of an answer and just relied on their standard reply of last resort: "It's ultimately a question of faith."

I was becoming disillusioned with the Church in many ways. I observed prominent people in the community who, in my estimation, acted notoriously improper or immoral, who would go to confession, attend church, accept Holy Communion, and then just go back to their wicked ways without any embarrassment, conscientiousness, or remorse.

I witnessed brothers and priests who looked down on and pontificated to people and then appeared to act as badly or even worse.

I was expected to confess my sins to priests because they were venerable members of the Church, notwithstanding that I considered them to be no more sacred or worthy than the average person.

I was infuriated with the Church's rules that changed over time, reportedly on the basis that the Church was keeping with the times when, in fact, it appeared they were merely seeking to maintain their relevancy in a modern society.

The apparent backflips included the previous prohibition from profiteering on loans, the once-accepted position on slavery, the former acceptance of capital punishment, and the original belief in the existence of Limbo. And what do all these changes suggest about the infallibility of the Pope?

I was frustrated how the Church's influence in the world seemed to create so much social upheaval, and was the cause of unnecessary suffering, even costing lives. These included the position it held on euthanasia, masturbation, abortion, premarital sex, homosexuality, artificial contraception, and the indissolubility of consummated sacramental marriage.

I was also perplexed by the Church's contradictions. How the Church could run large businesses and accumulate so much wealth when the scriptures echoed a different message. It is supposed to be more blessed to give than to receive, states *Acts 20:35*. *Proverb 28:27* states that whoever gives to the poor will not want, but those who hide their eyes to the poor will be cursed. More explicitly and unambiguously, *Matthew 19:24*, *Mark 10:25*, and *Luke 18:25* all state that Jesus said, it is easier for a camel to go through the eye of a needle than for a rich man to enter the kingdom of God.

I attended mass every Sunday until I was 16, usually with Michael and sometimes with Jessica and her friends. I normally attended the 9.00 a.m. Sunday service, while Joe took Mary to the Italian mass at 11.00 a.m.

I appreciated that mass was the rite inspired by the Last Supper, that remembered Christ's sacrifice and celebrated Christ's resurrection. I also recognised that mass brought the community together. Nonetheless, I was finding the services more and more boring.

Michael and I were chatting in the narthex of the church when Father Ryan walked by and angrily castigated us for talking. I looked around the entrance area, where there were other people also engaged in discussion, who were now looking at us in tense silence. I was tempted to react, but I thought better of it.

Michael and I attended mass the following Sunday, when Father Ryan was the celebrant. The service had reached the point where the parishioners were giving the sign of peace when the priest took to the microphone.

"If you are going to talk during mass," Father Ryan stated, "then you can leave."

Father Ryan was looking in the direction of those

of us seated in the left transept, but nobody moved, as we were unsure to whom he was referring. "I'm talking to you boys over there," he clarified as he pointed his finger in our direction.

There were about half a dozen boys in our area, and we still weren't sure who he was targeting; however, this didn't concern Michael and me. We had both had enough and were happy to leave, and neither of us ever returned for Sunday service.

"It's a pity not going to church anymore," Michael said.

"Why," I replied.

"Well, I still consider myself religious," Michael explained. "Now I can't practice it anymore."

I looked at Michael with a puzzled expression. "Of course you can practice your religion," I said. "Your religion doesn't exist because of the Church; it exists because of your belief in God."

"But if I don't go to mass and practice my religion, how can I follow the will of God?"

"Mass and all the practices aren't products of God," I opined. "They're rules and rites created by man over many years through the order of the Roman Catholic Church, just like any other religious order. Religion is one's personal relationship with God, and a person can talk to God wherever and whenever they want through prayer."

"I guess that's true," Michael said. "So why did we bother to go to mass every week?"

"To keep our parents happy," I replied, and then I

gasped. "Oh no! What am I going to tell my mum?"

# Chapter 19

## Agoraphobia

I drove Joe's car on my first day of university. It took one and a half hours from our house in Brunswick, north of Melbourne, to the campus situated 25 kilometres away in the south-eastern suburbs.

Dad wasn't thrilled I opted for that university, as he suggested I should attend the university closer to home. However, I wasn't keen on the idea of a compulsory sandwich year and the university I had selected had the most highly rated business school in the state.

I parked Joe's car in The Bog, which was a vacant site of undulating terrain where students could park all day for free. Needless to say, when it rained, the car park turned into a real bog.

I checked out my classes and planned my schedule for the first semester. I managed to cram all my tutorials and lectures into three contact days. Dad was kind enough to arrange his affairs to fit in with mine so I could use his car.

I was delighted to accompany Mary to do the shopping every week. On one occasion, we had parked in the supermarket car park and I had my head in the boot, placing the groceries in it, when I noticed Mary dart behind me. I swung around to see a car backing into me. Mary placed herself between me and the car as she waved her hand and shouted, "Stop!" As soon as the driver was alerted to the danger, he screeched on the brakes.

Mary still had one hand in the air and the other against the boot of the other car, which was inches away from her torso.

The driver scampered out of his vehicle. "Are you all right?" he asked fearfully, open-mouthed, his eyes bulging. "I'm sorry, but I didn't see you."

"I'm fine," Mary replied.

I was in horror as I realised that my mother had risked her safety to protect me. I always knew that she loved me and thought she would do anything for me; however, experiencing the reality rammed it home.

I hugged my mother as the man drove off. "Mum, you could have been hurt. Why did you do that?"

"I didn't use my head; I followed my heart," Mary replied. "And God is always looking after us."

I looked into her eyes and saw the purity of her faith as I reacted with a smile.

\*    \*    \*

Early morning every Friday, I accompanied Joe to the Queen Victoria Market. It was the one day of the week that I was excited to rise at 5.00 a.m. to secure our usual car park at the market by 6.00 a.m. Joe appeared like a celebrity as he visited his usual butchers, fishmongers, and greengrocers. There was always lively banter and Joe seemed proud to boast that his son was attending university.

Joe's standard purchases were fish for Fridays, rabbit for stew on Saturdays, and chicken for the Sunday roasts. In addition to oranges, bananas, apples, and pears, he bought cherries, because they were good for the heart, and grapes, because they were the Queen of Fruits.

*    *    *

Getting used to university life was proving the most difficult transition of my education. There was no one I knew and I had difficulty making new friends. The cultural environment was unique to me, with a mixture of ethnic backgrounds, but the most striking differences were my exposure to non-Catholic religions and, even stranger, people who were secular.

Furthermore, I had not been at a coeducational institution since primary school. My accounting course had few females, although other courses had lots. The marketing course, in particular, contained a bevy of young women, some of whom were stunningly attractive. One young lady simply took my breath away. She had fine, silky, blonde hair, cut in a bobby style. Her eyes were deep blue and she had a slim, petite body.

*Thank goodness I don't have that captivating young lady in any of my classes,* I thought. *I'd never be able to concentrate on my studies.*

I robotically attended my classes, arriving early and waiting for someone to sit next to me. The tutorials were smaller classes, where the students engaged in discussion. On the other hand, the lectures had many more students and were conducted in large auditoriums where there was minimal interaction.

\*     \*     \*

As I struggled to make new friends at university, I was heartened that Lou and Michael maintained social contact with me, notwithstanding that Lou was commencing an engineering apprenticeship and Michael had gained a retail traineeship.

Lou invited me to his house most Sundays, where there were smallish gatherings of around a dozen females and males. We watched *Countdown* on television at 6.00 p.m., enjoying the latest music from Australia and around the globe.

Every so often, Lou also invited me to go along with his family to attend the Veneto Club. We enjoyed dinner, which was followed by dancing. Lou's mother and father were among the first to hit the dance floor, while Lou, his younger sister, Lisa, and I sat back to admire them. Lou was soon off to pursue his favourite lady friends and I would be left with his sister.

Lisa was a 17-year-old, attractive girl with blonde hair and baby-blue eyes. She was a delightful girl and we got on well together as she seemed to be as shy as I was. We would go through a standard procedure whereby we both acted coy and then one of us would eventually ask the other for a dance. We would normally time it perfectly so that by the end of our dance it was time to reunite with the family for the drive home.

Michael and I had a mutual passion for rock music and we would habitually meet up on Friday and Saturday nights to go to pubs and clubs to hear live bands. Michael had many connections and he often got into the VIP areas, where he would hook up with girls while I simply tagged along.

Michael also invited me to parties with his traineeship friends, as well as a load of young cashiers and retail saleswomen. As usual, Michael was the centre of attention and I just went along for the ride.

Lou and Michael always scored with the women, which I completely understood, given their bubbly personalities and good looks. I also understood why I was always in the background and attracted little attention. However, what I didn't comprehend was why they bothered to go out of their way to invite me along. I mean, it was not as if they needed me.

What I found even more unusual was why Michael often invited me when he went out on a date. Honestly, wasn't three a crowd? Bizarrely, I actually went along.

After a considerable period of consternation, I simply had to ask them, "Why?"

"We enjoy your company," Lou said.

I stared at him in disbelief.

"It's true," Michael confirmed. "Our friends like you."

I turned to Michael and gave him a sterner stare, unconvinced. "Listen guys," I stated firmly. "We're long-time friends and you know I don't like to bullshit around, so why don't you just admit that you feel sorry for me."

"That's not true," Lou was quick to argue. "In fact, it was the girls who asked whether you were going to come, as they wanted to see you."

"That's right," Michael confirmed. "They find you interesting and they enjoy your jokes."

I gave them both a serious glare before I spoke. "I guess I am interesting to talk to, when people get to know me, and I do have a clever wit."

"By the way," Michael said. "Katie and I are going to the Kiss concert and she wants you to come."

"I guess I can't disappoint my fans," I quipped.

On Saturday 15 November 1980, I heard the familiar sound of a loud rumble coming around corner, which was Michael's Ford Falcon GT. He popped his head out of the driver's seat window and I hopped in the front passenger seat. Michael picked up Katie on the way.

"You don't have to get out of the front seat,"

Katie said. "I'm happy to sit in the back."

"I was actually getting out in the hope I'd pile in the back with you," I joked, and we all laughed. "Go on, Katie, take the front," I insisted. "Then I can give Michael a clip behind the ear when he misbehaves."

"Good idea," Katie replied as she stepped into the front seat with a beaming smile.

We were highly excited as we made the long drive to Waverley Park to see Kiss as part of their *Unmasked* tour. By the time we settled in, the support band, Eyes, were playing. There was great anticipation ahead of the main act and the buzz of the crowd was building.

Kiss finally made the stage and the crowd erupted, with the noise not letting up for their complete set. There were many special effects and enormous fireworks as the band left the stage.

Katie, Michael, and I looked to one another as the fireworks wound up and smoke lingered around us. The feeling amongst the three of us was unanimous: we all thought the concert was a fizzer.

I considered that the event was symbolic, as it seemed to be the catalyst for our friendship to wane.

Eventually, I lost contact with both Lou and Michael, as I had done with all my previous friends from primary and secondary school. Lou moved on to concentrate on his apprenticeship and Michael pursued his traineeship. I was saddened by this, but I recognised that I also had to move on and follow the path leading to my future.

*    *    *

Jessica was completing her Diploma of Education while I ploughed through my first year of university. Even though I was 18, she was still looking out for me.

We had a close-knit family and had continued the tradition of having dinner together, although Jessica was drawn away more and more. She was building up a wide circle of friends and attending more varied social events.

Jessica appreciated my difficulties in making the transition to university life and finding new friends, particularly since I had distanced myself from my previous companions. I hardly ever went out, so she started inviting me to some of her social engagements.

I was grateful for her kind invitations, but I declined. After a few weeks of not going out, even my parents expressed concern.

"Why don't you go out with your sister?" Mary would ask. "It couldn't do you any harm."

"You never know, you might even find a nice girl," Joe suggested.

I mulled over the idea for some time and when Jessica asked me to accompany her to a small gathering with her friends, I eventually relented.

Jessica drove us to the event, which was in a small house in the northern suburb of Northcote. It was a cool evening, but as we entered the house, we were met with a warm surge of body heat and cigarette smoke, and a loud babble of numerous voices talking over one another.

I found it a chaotic scene and, in an effort to get used to the surroundings, I took a few gasps for air and tried to shut out the noise. Jessica handed me a beer and introduced me to a few of her friends before she wandered off.

I was left with two young women and a young man who were going on and on about their practical experiences in teaching, which I soon found utterly boring. My contribution to the conversation was an odd smile and the occasional nod.

I gazed around the room to observe the activities and was admiring the pretty young women when I sensed the heat and noise in the room increase in intensity. I was acutely conscious of the voices coming from different directions and started turning my head to follow the sounds as I picked up on them.

The numerous voices then blended into an incoherent cacophony and the movement of the people seemed to be in slow motion. It was the first time I had ever felt like I was having an out-of-body experience.

I was frightened and tried to snap out of it by focussing on the group of people around me, but they were engaged in fervid conversation and seemed to be completely oblivious to my existence.

All of a sudden, I started to perspire profusely and was having trouble breathing. I began to pant in an effort to catch my breath, but it didn't work and it got to the point where I felt I was about to faint, so I rushed out of the house to get some air.

After I composed myself, I re-entered the room and immediately felt the same uncomfortable sensations coming on again. I quickly sought out Jessica and informed her I was heading off.

"Wait," Jessica said. "I'll give you a lift."

"No, I'll be fine," I replied. "I might check out a few places before I go home."

"Okay," Jessica said as she gave me a kiss on the cheek. "Take care."

I was greatly relieved when I escaped the scene and strolled the streets, taking deep breaths. I ended up walking the six kilometres home and then went straight to bed. I lay there with my eyes wide open in pitch darkness, trying to comprehend what had happened.

Jessica invited me to a number of other social events, but I was reluctant, if not scared, to go.

A few weeks went by, during which time I hadn't gone out, Jessica queried what was wrong. I struggled to provide a convincing reason for my seclusion and so, when she invited me to another small gathering at a private house, I accepted.

Jessica drove us again, this time to a Victorian cottage in Fitzroy, an inner northern suburb of Melbourne. We walked down a long corridor and entered the living room, where there were only a dozen or so people.

I recognised a couple of women Jessica had previously introduced to me. Jessica handed me a beer, sipped on champagne, and engaged in some light conversation before she went off to mingle. I was left with a few of her friends.

I felt reasonably comfortable, although I found the discussion uninspiring. They seemed to be utterly obsessed with teaching.

As the evening progressed, more and more people turned up and encroached on me. I felt a crowd crush and noticed the noise, the smoke, and the body heat. I started to perspire and breathe heavily. I tried to compose myself, but it appeared I had lost control of my senses.

I rushed to find the toilet and locked the door behind me. I took a few deep breaths and spent some time there in an effort to relax. I still didn't feel comfortable, so I located Jessica to let her know I was leaving.

"Are you all right?" Jessica asked me.

"Yeah, I'm fine."

"You don't look too good," she remarked. "I'll drive you home."

"I never look good," I said with a smile. "I'm absolutely fine and I'd prefer to head off by myself."

Jessica appeared unconvinced, but she let me go. "Take care," she said. "And come back if you want a lift."

I was instantly relieved when I exited the house. I took in the clear night air, walked the seven kilometres home, and went straight to bed.

After my previous experiences, I was loath to go out to any social event. Despite my sister's encouragement and support, I declined all invitations. Nearing the end of 1980, Jessica enquired what I was doing for New Year's Eve.

"Nothing," was my curt reply.

"You simply must come to a small New Year's Eve party," Jessica said in a high-spirited, upbeat voice. "It's going to be a costume party!"

"I don't think so."

"You have to come," she insisted. "My friends can't make it and I'll hardly know anyone, so I'd really feel better if someone I knew was with me."

I carefully inspected her countenance, trying to figure out whether she was sincere, but all I saw was a young woman with puppy-dog eyes and a hopeful smile.

"What are you going as?" I asked her.

"It's a horror theme," Jessica explained. "So I was thinking of going as Morticia Addams from *The Addams Family*."

"That sounds good."

"Maybe you could come as Dracula."

"I don't know," I said, as I momentarily reflected on it. "I'll think about it and let you know."

Days later, I was relaxing in my room when Jessica burst in. "What do you think of this?"

It took me a few seconds to gather myself and focus on her. She was wearing a tight-fitting, black hobble dress with a long, sweeping train.

"It's Morticia Addams, I presume."

"That's right. What do you think?"

"I think it actually looks good."

"Look what else I've bought," Jessica stated with glee as she pulled out a set of fangs and a black cape.

"Why did you buy those?" I asked. "I didn't say I'd come."

"It's okay. They didn't cost much. Go on. Try them on."

"I don't feel like it."

"Well, I'll leave them here and you can try them later."

Jessica left and I looked at the items placed on my bed from a distance. I walked around my room for a while before my resistance gave way and I picked up the vampire upper teeth. They slipped in easily and fit me perfectly.

I looked in the mirror and was astounded with the transformation. The teeth had pushed up my upper lip and gave me a smile — one you could actually see. I had also grown my hair long, so my ears were not visible.

I took off my pullover, draped the cape over my shoulders, and fastened it at the neck. With my gaze fixed on the mirror, I raised my arms to expose the outline of my body against the red lining of the cape. I visualised my metamorphosis into a ghostly fiend and thought I had never looked more normal.

I joined my family for dinner and Jessica kept

glancing at me without saying a word. I eventually returned her look. "Okay, I'll come."

Jessica drove us to the party, which was in a two-story Victorian terrace in the nearby suburb of North Fitzroy. I got out the car, collected my cape from the back seat, draped it across my shoulders, and fastened it. I then slipped in my Dracula teeth.

Jessica had to pull down her tight-fitting dress before she could manage to wobble towards the house. I followed her and when we got to the front door, we were held up on the veranda as a crowd of people caused a bottleneck in the corridor.

After several minutes, Jessica managed to squeeze through. I trailed her with great apprehension and took a few deep breaths as we moved down the corridor and into the living room.

The area was full of people and I felt cramped. As usual, Jessica managed to find the drinks and was soon sipping on a glass of champagne as she handed me a beer.

"Are you okay?" Jessica asked me.

I was uneasy and was about to utter a negative reply, when I caught sight of a stunning creature. Our eyes met and there seemed to be an immediate connection.

The woman appeared to float towards me as the crowd parted to make way for her. She wore a floor-length, tight, black velvet dress that had an off-shoulder crossover neckline with a matching studded leather belt. Her makeup was classic goth, with pale white skin, black eye shadow, and blood-red lipstick. She appeared a perfect specimen of womanhood, with an hour-glass figure, cute turned-up nose, dark-brown eyes, and natural black hair.

Jessica, like many of the crowd, noticed the woman's approach. "I'll see you later," Jessica whispered in my ear as she whisked herself away.

"You must be Count Dracula," the woman stated.

"Yes," I replied. "I am the Count."

"How can I be sure you're a real count?"

"Oh, I'm a real count all right. In fact, when people write to me or write about me, they always refer to me as a count, although they all seem to be atrocious spellers, as they always leave out the 'o'."

The woman smiled.

"And who might you be?" I asked.

"I'm Vampira, of course."

"Vampira? I thought Vampira was black."

"You're probably referring to the appalling 1974 spoof movie with a black actress; however, the original Vampira is white."

"I appreciate the clarification," I said. "Fangs for that."

Vampira rolled her eyes. "I hope you're not going to make those silly Dracula jokes all night?"

"Of course not. Although I have to say that this beer sucks."

"I suspect you'd prefer a Bloody Mary."

"Not necessarily. I don't discriminate. It doesn't have to be Mary; it can be a bloody anyone."

At this point, Vampira opened up with delightful laughter.

After a while, as time was creeping on, I expected Vampira would want to move on, but she continued to hang around me.

"It's approaching midnight," I pointed out. "Don't you want to catch up with your friends?"

"Why, Count? You aren't trying to get rid of me, are you?"

"No, not at all. I just thought you might prefer to catch up with other people."

"Don't you think I'd be happy to stay with you?"

"I wouldn't have thought so."

"Why?"

"After a while, most people find me to be a pain in the neck."

We both laughed as the countdown to midnight was upon us. We looked into each other's eyes, and she exposed her teeth and pointed to them.

"What?" I asked.

"Take out your fangs."

I took them out, and she planted a passionate kiss on me. I felt a surge of pulsating delight radiate through my body. When she pulled away, she wished me Happy New Year.

I quickly replaced my false teeth to re-establish my mask. "Happy New Year to you too," I said in a ghoulish voice and smiled, showing off my gleaming false teeth.

Vampira and I kept each other company as the

crowd diminished and I was reunited with Jessica.

"Hello," Jessica said. "I was about to go, so did you want a lift?"

I looked to Vampira. "Do you need a ride?"

"Oh, no," Vampira replied. "I've already got one."

"Okay," I said, and then hesitated. "Well, goodbye."

"Goodbye," Vampira said, and she gave me a peck on the cheek.

Again, a surge of delight radiated through my body and then I left.

"That woman was really beautiful," Jessica remarked as we were driving home. "What was her name?"

"Vampira."

"No, what was her real name."

"I don't know," I replied, and then I thought, *I spent most of the night with Vampira and I didn't even have the courtesy to ask her real name. I did the same thing my first time. What is wrong with me?*

# Chapter 20

## My University Days

Jessica had completed her studies and was looking forward to her first teaching position, but even more significantly, she was overjoyed with the anticipation of her imminent wedding.

After a period of dating, she was thrilled to have the pledge of love from her favourite suitor, Beau. It was to be a brief engagement with an autumn wedding. Joe and Mary shared Jessica's excitement, while I was indifferent.

It was a small wedding for close family and friends. I was tentative about the occasion, but the VIP treatment I received from being in the wedding party, aided by copious amounts of alcohol, allowed me to relax and have a marvellous time.

Soon after and also at short notice, my parents revealed they were going on holiday to their home country — Italy — within a few months. When Jessica left the family home, I felt a little stranded, but when my parents departed on their three-month trip, I felt abandoned.

Jessica had left home in May and my parents departed Australia in July. I had passed my first year of university and the first semester of my second year, but from the beginning of the second semester, I rapidly took a downward spiral and the impact on me was devastating.

I was home alone and still hadn't made any friends. I replaced proper meals with snacks and alcohol. I travelled three to four hours every school day, but otherwise never went out. Whereas study had once provided me with a preoccupation and refuge, I now found it impossible to maintain my concentration. I had effectively turned into a recluse.

Early into the second semester, I was getting up late and had missed a number of classes in all my four subjects. The university was surrounded by snack bars and pubs, in which I spent more time than I did in tutorial rooms and lecture halls.

At lunch, I would habitually go to the corner store across the road from the university, grab some fast food, and munch on it while playing the pin ball machines and *Pac-Man*. The most popular pin ball machine was *Charlie's Angels*, but my favourite was *Eight Ball Deluxe*. I always got a kick out of hearing the recorded voice, particularly when it stated, "Stop talking and start chalking."

One day when I entered the university cafeteria there was a group of students, mainly of Greek ethnic background, playing cards. I noticed that, at the end of each hand, money was exchanged. Ironically, there was a sign stuck on the wall directly above them that read: No gambling allowed.

One of the guys looked at me. "Do you have a problem?"

"No," I replied. "Although, I was wondering whether you were aware of the sign."

"Of course we are," another guy responded. "That's exactly why we sit here."

"Rebels with a cause," I remarked with a smile.

"We're playing Manila," the first guy advised. "Do you want to play?"

"No thanks. I don't know how to play Manila, but I do know that cards is a fast way to lose money. Do you mind if I watch?"

"Go ahead," the first guy said.

"Yeah, take a seat," the second guy added.

I took a seat next to a couple of other observers.

"Hi. My name's Heston and this is Spiro," one of the observers said as he shook my hand.

"Hi. I'm Frank. Do you guys play?"

"No way," Spiro said. "These guys bet big and, you're right, it is a fast way to lose money."

Over the course of the next few weeks, I ascertained that Heston and Spiro were undertaking the same course as I and took many of my classes. They also introduced me to their other two friends, Theo and Matt.

I got on well with the group and, as I gained their trust, I gradually joined them. It was a rude awakening when they filled me in on what I had missed by being absent from so many classes.

In the Cost Accounting subject, I hadn't been

placed in a work group, which was a requirement to undertake a project. On learning this, I immediately approached the teacher to inform him.

"You're really in a difficult situation," Mr Moyle said. "All the other students have been placed in groups and have been working on their projects for a few weeks, so it would be unfair to place you in a group now."

"So what can I do?"

"You could withdraw," Mr Moyle suggested. "Although, given the time that has elapsed, it will show up as a fail."

"I wouldn't want to do that," I said. "Is there some other way? I'd be prepared to do anything."

Mr Moyle ummed and ahed before saying to leave it with him.

At the end of the next tutorial, Mr Moyle pulled me aside. "I've considered your situation and the only offer I can make is for you to undertake a research paper of about 10,000 words based on an area I'm particularly interested in, which is departmental costing."

"Absolutely," I instantly replied.

"Okay then. I'll provide you with a brief and you can get on with it straightaway."

"Thank you, sir; I really appreciate this."

Mr Moyle provided scant information in the brief and minimal guidance. I immediately got to work on the research paper and, as I made enquiries at the library, was curious to learn that the topic of departmental costing had been a bugbear of Mr Moyle's for some time.

I was about four weeks behind in all four subjects, so I made a concerted effort to catch up. *It's just like my Higher School Certificate year all over again,* I thought. *I guess I'll never learn.*

With only a couple of weeks until the examinations and a few weeks until the end of semester, I made a point of providing Mr Moyle with a draft of my research paper.

"I'm very concerned about this paper," Mr Moyle commented after he had read it.

I was taken aback. "What's wrong with it?"

"The paper provides great detail and is of such a high standard that I question whether it is your work."

I was completely dumbfounded. "I don't understand," I said, with a slight quiver in my voice. "Every single piece of information I took from sources has been referenced and footnoted."

"Well, I'm still concerned," Mr Moyle said as he sighed and leaned back in his armchair. "I'll tell you what I want you to do. I want you to complete the paper and highlight every word that has come from other sources and every word that comes from you."

I gazed at him, wondering what sort of imbecile he was, but I replied in a defiant tone. "Okay. I'll do as you say."

As silly as I thought the instructions Mr Moyle gave me, I had not fully appreciated the difficulty in having to compare every word in my paper against the more than one hundred sources, as well as figuring out how I would deal with the parts I had paraphrased. In the end, I effectively undertook a complete re-write where I identified everything.

I put my all into the task, but it took an inordinate amount of time and caused me to neglect my other subjects. I was grossly underprepared and distraught as I sat my exams. It was a feeling I knew well and I hoped for the best.

The last duty I had to perform that semester was to hand in my research paper. When I entered Mr Moyle's office, he was seated and appeared chuffed. I remained standing and took out two documents from my bag.

"I assume that's your research paper," he said.

"Yes, sir. One is a copy of the research paper marked up as instructed and the other is a clean copy."

"Thanks, Frank. I wish you luck."

I was in the university cafeteria mulling over my research paper when the gang — Heston, Spiro, Theo, and Matt — entered. They were in high spirits and laughing out loud. As soon as they noticed me, they came over.

"You look worried," Matt observed. "What's up?"

"I was just thinking about that stupid research paper."

"I'm sure you'll be all right," Heston remarked.

"I don't know about that," Spiro said. "Mr Moyle

can be a bit of a dickhead."

"That's not what I want to hear," I said.

"At least we're sure to get good marks for Business Statistics," Matt suggested.

"Why do you say that?" I asked, while the others looked at me, confused. "I thought the exam was pretty tricky."

Heston seemed particularly concerned. "Well, we were virtually given the answers," he advised.

"What are you talking about?"

"Mr Brady handed out mock essays and multiple-choice questions from previous years and indicated where the answers could be located in the library," Theo advised.

"Actually, I was sort of embarrassed at getting all the answers right in the multiple choice," Spiro added. "So I purposely got a couple wrong."

"I can't believe you guys didn't tell me this before!"

"We assumed you knew," Heston said. "I'm sure you'll be all right."

In despair, I put my elbows on the table and placed my head in my hands.

The results for the semester came through and I impassively opened the envelop to reveal my grades. I achieved a credit for Organisational Behaviour & Performance and a pass for Corporate Law. I was unfazed at having failed Business Statistics, but I was astonished I had also failed Cost Accounting. The only scintilla of solace was the news that Spiro had also failed Business Statistics.

I was philosophical about my disastrous assessment, but it was a gigantic wakeup call. I withheld the information from my parents and caught up on my failed subjects by adding an extra one in each of the two semesters of my last year. Notwithstanding the heavier workload, I managed to achieve a credit in every subject.

# Chapter 21

## Campus Interviews

During my time at university, I funded myself through weekend work as a factory hand, casual labouring jobs, and full-time seasonal work for a couple of months each year over the Christmas period, at penalty rates, with the General Post Office as a mail sorter or handling mail bags.

I was grateful to undertake the more physically demanding work as it provided me with the greatest incentive to pursue higher education for a better life.

I also managed to save sufficient money to purchase my first car: a yellow panel van, also known as a shaggin' wagon. In fact, shagging was the last thing on my mind when I bought the van; my plan was to use it to travel around Australia.

I attended half a dozen campus interviews, mostly with highly rated accounting firms, but I was unimpressed by all of them.

I made my way to the meeting room for my penultimate interview and arrived just before the scheduled time. I quickly adjusted my tie and was about to take a seat in the waiting area when an elderly man approached and invited me to enter.

The man was wearing a brown sports coat with light-brown elbow patches and an open-necked shirt.

We engaged in social conversation, which seemed appropriate given my apathetic mood and, as I felt, that of the interviewer.

After about half an hour, there was a long pause, and I reflected on how wishy-washy the whole interview had been.

"So, is that it from your end?" I asked nonchalantly.

"I think so," the elderly gentlemen answered.

I felt I couldn't possibly leave the interview on such a sober note. "Sir, let me say that this has been an absolute pleasure and I would be highly honoured if I could be considered to join such a fine establishment as the Tax Office."

I offered the man my hand and, as he took hold, I initiated an enthusiastic handshake. The interviewer seemed genuinely inspired, and I left the room.

I made my way to the university cafeteria, found a vacant table, and took a seat. Soon after, I heard footsteps heading in my direction and I glanced up. "Hi, Heston. How's it going?"

"I just had my last interview," Heston informed me. "It was with the Audit Office and I think I did okay."

"If you get the job, wouldn't that mean you'd have to go to Canberra?"

"That's true," Heston confirmed. "But the word is you can usually get back to Melbourne after the first year's training."

"One whole year in that artificial city," I said, shaking my head. "I wouldn't like the prospect of spending that long in such a sterile place."

"I don't know about that. Apparently it's a bit of a holiday. So, how did your interview go?"

"It was with the Tax Office and was completely underwhelming. I left the interview thinking that there was one place I definitely would not want to work."

"Yeah, I had an interview with them and I know what you mean. I'm sure you'll find your interview with the Audit Office slightly more professional," Heston suggested in an upbeat voice.

I was making my way to my last interview when Heston pulled me up. "By the way," he said. "They'll probably ask whether you'd mind working in Canberra and it's probably not a good idea to say you wouldn't want to work in such an artificial city."

"Gotcha," I said with a smile.

Arriving at the interview room, I took a seat in the waiting area. Fifteen minutes later, the interview room door opened and a man waved me inside

I entered the room to be greeted by two men wearing designer suits. Both appeared middle-aged and they were seated on one side of the table. One of the men invited me to take a seat across from them.

The interview commenced with some brief introductions and proceeded with a number of technical questions. I was reasonably comfortable with my responses, although I became a little fidgety at the next question.

"The position is posted in Canberra, so what is your attitude to working there?"

"Well, to be perfectly honest," I said as I looked to the heavens. "I've heard varying reports, so it's hard to anticipate how I would feel about working in Canberra. However, I'd certainly be keen to take up an opportunity that may result in a rewarding, long-term career."

The men looked at each other, but I couldn't garner any sign of how my response had been received.

"Thank you for your candour," said the man who'd asked the question. "That concludes the interview and you will be notified in due course."

I completed my last stint working at the General Post Office during the time before the Christmas of 1981.

I spent New Year's Eve at a party in Melbourne CBD with Heston, Theo, Matt, and Spiro. We migrated between the indoor restaurant and the al fresco smoking area. We were juggling our drinks and smokes as we engaged numerous women in various forms of conversation, from playful palaver to stimulating repartee. It was an enjoyable event and I thought a good way to top-off my university days.

# Chapter 22

## An Artificial City

It was early in 1982 when letters with job offers were delivered. Heston gained a job at the Tax Office and I received a job offer from the Audit Office. Ironically, both positions were in Canberra.

Theo got an exciting position as a film accountant through a friend of his family, Matt took up a position in his father's import-export business, while Spiro was still completing his university course.

Heston and I commenced our positions with our respective employers in February 1982. We separately made our way to Canberra, with me driving my panel van — the shaggin' wagon.

Heston and I had similar arrangements whereby the government organised accommodation for the first three weeks and provided travel allowances.

Heston was housed in Macquarie Hostel, located on National Circuit at Barton, while I ended up at the exceptionally basic Gowrie Hostel on Northbourne Avenue at Turner. Just to rub it in, my accommodation was directly across the road from the Canberra Rex Hotel — 'the luxury hotel'.

The first three weeks in the Audit Office went by

in the blink of an eye. I managed to find longer-term accommodation with three co-workers at Kaleen, north of the city centre.

Heston also found accommodation with three of his co-workers at Kingston, south of the city centre and conveniently close to Fyshwick, famous for firecrackers and porn.

During my probation period, I had four separate placements in four separate buildings: Cameron Offices at Belconnen, Canberra House at Civic, the Treasury Building at Parkes, and the National Gallery building.

My housemates and I met up with Heston and his housemates just about every day. There was a vibrant social scene and we frequented the many pubs and clubs that Canberra had to offer.

Every Friday after work, we gravitated to a nominated pub. There were various venues, each with its own appeal. One pub was especially popular as there were scantily dressed barmaids. The place would be packed with eager patrons as it neared 6.00 p.m., at which time the dress code was relaxed and the waitresses went around topless.

Saturday nights were usually reserved for the nightclubs, which was the main time when we enjoyed the company of the opposite sex. They were debaucherous affairs where we drank and danced the night away. We were usually so sloshed by the end of the night that we struggled to make it back to our accommodation. As much fun as we had socialising, the boys rarely picked up a girl and I never did.

In December 1982, after 10 months in Canberra, I gained a graduate position to complete the final two months of my probation. I was delighted to learn the placement was in the Melbourne regional office.

Heston's probation period spanned 12 months in Canberra and until the Tax Office placements were determined sometime in early 1983, he had no idea where he would end up.

After farewelling Heston and all my friends in Canberra, I reflected on the fun times I'd had and felt a hint of regret. However, as I gained distance from the artificial city and neared Melbourne, I looked forward to my future career and was increasingly excited at the thought of reuniting with my parents.

I had rung my parents every week during my time in Canberra and, during the last call, I had given them an estimated time for my arrival. As I turned into our street, I saw a familiar figure. Joe waved his arm and he was soon joined by Mary. They were both waiting for me, wearing beaming smiles, as I parked in front of the family home.

Mary embraced me while Joe stood back, but as soon as Mary had curbed her hugs and kisses, Joe shook my hand and welcomed me home.

I settled into my room, which appeared much smaller than I remembered. I finished unpacking as the clock ticked over to 6.00 p.m. and then I heard my dad's customary cry: "It's time for the news!"

As I walked through the kitchen where Mary was

preparing dinner, she pulled me up and gave me another hug and kiss before I moved into the lounge.

Joe was seated in his beloved recliner and I took a seat on the couch. I looked at my dad and then I looked to where Jessica used to sit.

Joe seemed to notice my movement, as he also looked in that direction. We then glanced at each other and exchanged ironic smiles.

# Chapter 23

## Audit Office Melbourne

I felt strange as I prepared for work. I was going to a new job in a new building where, as far as I was aware, I didn't know anyone. It was as if I was commencing my career all over again.

I made final adjustments to my suit and tie before I bid my parents goodbye. I caught the number 55 tram, just as I had done when I attended my last two years of secondary school.

I got off the tram in the city centre and weaved my way through the streets of the Melbourne CBD until I reached my destination, being the headquarters of the Melbourne regional office in the Bureau of Meteorology building at 150 Lonsdale Street, Melbourne.

The regional office in Melbourne was organised into nine sections comprising seven field sections, a specialist Information Technology Section, and a Management Service Section for administrative support to professional staff.

The Melbourne Audit Office's audit portfolio included statutory authorities with their head offices in Melbourne, departmental commercial undertakings located in Victoria, and departments with large-scale operations throughout the state.

Each field section was allocated a range of government departments, statutory authorities, and government-owned or government-controlled companies. The auditors had the responsibility to conduct regularity audits (comprising financial statements audits, government accounting audits, and other regularity audits) and performance audits (comprising efficiency audits and project audits).

The field audit sections adopted flexible accommodation arrangements in order to adapt to their particular audit assignments and locations. I was assigned to a field section located in another CBD office building and I set off to track it down.

I eventually located my section and presented myself to the section leader, Mr Meaney.

The field section comprised a dozen staff with five Senior Auditors and five Auditors. I was the lowest-level staff member, being the only graduate. Other than the sole woman in the section, it was a motley group of males of varying ages and experience.

After brief introductions to the rest of the section, and an even briefer summary of the work they were undertaking, I was shown to my desk and allowed to settle in.

It wasn't long before I heard a rattling that caused a stir amongst the staff. It was the arrival of the tea trolley and there was a mad rush to be first in line.

The tea trolley had two large metal urns, one for

coffee and one for tea. There was also a selection of snacks, including coffee scrolls, hot cross buns, cream buns, chips, chocolate bars, and cold drinks.

During the bustle, a young man tentatively approached me and introduced himself as Bill.

"It's always the same guys first in line for the tea trolley, usually the managers," Bill explained. "The official time for tea breaks is 15 minutes, but the unofficial practice is that the time starts from when the last person is served. This usually results in morning and afternoon tea breaks of around 30 minutes or even longer."

Bill turned his attention to my desk, which was of solid timber with a green plastic writing surface and two large drawers on either side. "Every desk is equipped with an ash tray, of course," he said as he strode off to buy a coffee.

I followed Bill across the shiny, immaculate linoleum floor to the tea trolley and was the last customer with my purchase of a coffee and a coffee scroll.

The staff in my section generally kept to themselves. I dutifully went about my work, although the final two months of my probation were not much more than a formality.

I had a quiet, but enjoyable, holiday period with my family, including Jessica and Beau, who joined us on Christmas Day and New Year's Day.

In February of 1983, I passed my probation and was promoted to the position of Auditor, Clerk Class

5.

Later in the month, I was stoked to learn that Heston had commenced a permanent position as a Tax Assessor, Clerk Class 2/3 in the Tax Office at 350 Collins Street, Melbourne.

The moment Heston returned to Melbourne, he attracted members of the group from our university days, with Theo, Matt, and even Spiro reuniting for drinks on Fridays after work.

It took a few months before I managed to develop a couple of friendships within the Audit Office, neither of whom were in my section.

Jim was a Senior Auditor in his 50s and generally described as 'old–school', although I considered him to be a true gentleman, so I nicknamed him Gentleman Jim.

Ron was an Auditor a few years older than I who was exceptionally selfless and helpful.

The three of us developed a close bond and regularly met for lunch. I found them both to be highly supportive. I also appreciated that neither ever called me names or made any derogatory comments.

I was proud to be working as a public servant in the Federal Government, recognising that the auditing work provided a critical function for the community. However, I was disturbed about the developments of public sector auditing in Australia, as well as around the world. There was a worldwide trend to move from compliance audits to performance audits, or 'value for money' audits as they were known in Canada.

In Australia, the *Audit Act* was amended in 1979 to give the Audit Office the authority to conduct performance audits with the first efficiency audits tabled in 1980.

In 1983, the government released a White Paper on reforming the public service, which noted the need for a complete overhaul of the public service practice, with a shift in management emphasis from compliance to performance.

Within the Audit Office, these developments were of serious concern to both senior management and auditors alike. Their concerns could be detected in consecutive senior executive reports and their sentiments were also reflected in articles in the media.

One article, in particular, described how the Audit Office had a substantially increased workload with the requirement to undertake efficiency audits and other increased responsibilities, while being greatly understaffed, with fewer staff in 1984 than it had when the additional responsibilities were introduced back in 1979. However, the plight of the Audit Office fell on deaf ears. There were obviously grander designs at play, by more influential and powerful stakeholders.

Notwithstanding the apparent worldwide developments in the field of auditing, driven by political and industry leaders, our audit staff seemed to be neglected.

I personally experienced a lack of support when I

was interested in furthering my technical knowledge, but found there was limited opportunity to do so in the Audit Office. As such, in the first semester of 1984, I returned to university to commence a Graduate Diploma in Accounting.

In order to satisfy the government's public service reform demands, public service departments were required to make efficiency dividends, which essentially forced job cuts by stealth. As the functions of the Audit Office were still required, this opened the way for contracting out work.

The culmination of these factors resulted in the ridiculous situation in the Audit Office whereby the efficiencies demanded by the government were achieved by sacking Audit Office staff and paying private sector firms to do the work at a much greater overall cost.

\*     \*     \*

During the 1986-87 financial year, the Melbourne regional office relocated to 303 Collins Street, Melbourne, where we occupied the 3rd and 7th floors. If anything, the move was a pleasant distraction from the mounting headwinds that were being felt by the Audit Office and, in particular, its staff.

What was an even more pleasant surprise during 1987 was when Jessica announced she and Beau were expecting their first child, and, in September of that year, I became an uncle for the first time to a healthy baby boy named Milton.

*     *     *

The Audit Office was subjected to private enterprise competitive pressures, which resulted in government business enterprises being given the opportunity to recommend the choice of an external auditor instead of the Audit Office.

At the same time, the Audit Office was experiencing ongoing strict staff numbers and salary constraints, with staff turnover exceptionally high.

Ironically, the only visible response to the serious concerns raised by the Audit Office was to subject it to yet another inquiry by the Committee of Public Accounts.

The Audit Office auditors were externally, and unfairly, branded as being risk averse and accused of over-auditing. They alleged we focused too much on the examination of processes rather than on outcomes.

The public sector seemed to be pressured to move away from an input-oriented approach to a more flexible, output-oriented approach.

The government was pushing for these changes with the stated aim of improving the efficiency and effectiveness of government administration. Although I knew of no one in the Audit Office who honestly believed the proposed public service reform would achieve this objective.

Nevertheless, within its limited resources, Audit Office management recognised that the powers that be would expect nothing other than their support in the new approach. As a result, there was a move towards cutting red tape and devolving authority. However, in practice, cutting red tape was often just cutting corners, devolving authority was often just taking greater risks, and proper process and accountability was often sacrificed in order for the external auditors to churn out their dubious efficiency audits.

# Chapter 24

## An Overseas Adventure

I had been working at the Audit Office for six years. Morale in the office was low and getting worse. The direction the office was heading was a major concern to staff and I was not immune. I had become disillusioned and frustrated, and what made the situation feel dire was that there did not appear to be any light at the end of the tunnel.

I'd had designs to travel around Australia in my panel van, but it was something I was never going to do on my own, so I sold it. I hadn't had a proper break for a while and I had never had a decent holiday.

I trawled through a plethora of brochures, catalogues, and travel books, but I couldn't find anything that piqued my interest. I was thinking about ditching the idea when I remembered back to the time my parents went on their overseas holiday to Italy and the joy it brought them. I then had a light bulb moment and was overwhelmed with wanderlust.

I re-examined the same information as before, but now everything seemed interesting and exciting. Rather than not finding any of the tours appealing, I was now in a quandary to select the holiday I liked the most. I finally chose the trip that suited me best and worked out an itinerary.

The following week, I pulled my parents aside. "I've decided to take a four-month holiday in Europe," I informed them. I waited for a reaction, but they appeared impassive. "I've also set aside a few weeks to meet the relatives in Italy."

My parents looked at each other with mutual expressions of wonder, before Mary broke the silence. "That's terrific, Frank."

"Yes, that's great, son," Joe added. "I'm sure you'll have great time."

It wasn't long before the big day of my departure, 5 June 1988, arrived. I completed my packing and was ready ahead of schedule. My parents and I perched on the side of the bed in the front room, looking out for the taxi without uttering a word.

When the taxi arrived, Mary hugged and kissed me. Joe stood back, but as soon as Mary gave way, he moved to shake my hand, then pulled me close and hugged me instead. There was a quiet moment, which was broken when Joe yelled, "Hurry up before you miss your plane!"

It was a short taxi ride to the Melbourne International Airport terminal. I had some time before my flight, so I did some window shopping, examining merchandise that took my eye without any intention to buy.

When it was time to board, I joined the last

remaining passengers in the queue. I took my seat and shut out all surrounding noises. My thoughts were still with my parents.

It was a smooth flight, with a short stopover before the onward journey to London. Soon after the plane touched down at London Heathrow, I followed the other passengers and was confronted with three aisles: British, European, and Other. *So much for being part of the Commonwealth*, I thought. *Oh well, I'll just join the long line.*

After going through Immigration and Customs, I caught the train to Victoria Station and then weaved my way through the crowd to the taxi rank. I was thrilled to take a back seat in a classic London black cab.

I was nestled in my seat, open-mouthed, as I marvelled at the continuous stream of historic landmarks. The city was bustling and intense, with sounds amplified to levels I had never previously experienced. I was so unprepared for the onslaught of attractions that I was gobsmacked.

I checked into the Royal National Hotel and relaxed until late afternoon, when it was time for the tour's pre-departure meeting. By the time I found the designated room, I was ten minutes late and took one of the last remaining seats. One additional straggler joined the group, after which a man stood up.

"Hello everyone, my name is Martin, your tour guide. We've got a bit of stuff to cover, so we'd better make a start." Martin outlined instructions and provided information about the tour.

When Martin had completed the formalities, he offered an option for us to have dinner together. "It was difficult to arrange dinner anywhere other than at the hotel as it's such a large group," he explained. "There's a set menu of either meat or fish with fries, followed by dessert."

The four vegetarians politely declined, as did a number of others, which left about half the group who took up the dinner offer.

It was mid-evening by the time we sat for our meal and we wasted no time with the introductions and gossip. From what we could work out, there were 50 passengers comprising 2 couples, 39 single women, and only 7 single men.

"Gee guys, you'd better look out with this many women after you," one of the ladies joked and the others laughed.

After dinner, we wished one another goodnight ahead of our early morning start the following day.

When morning came, I took a seat towards the back of the bus and introduced myself to the man sitting next to me. His name was Max and he came across as a good-natured, happy-go-lucky type of guy.

The bus departed just as dawn broke and Martin allowed the driver to introduce himself. "Good morning everyone, my name is Scott, but most people call me Lanky." This was understandable as Lanky was tall, lean, and gangly. Martin, on the other hand, was short and pixie-looking.

As soon as Lanky finished his address, music started playing. It was Monty Python's 'Always Look on the Bright Side of Life', which was the tour theme song and it was an instant hit.

We drove to the port at Dover with lively chatter all the way. We then jumped on a ferry to cross the English Channel, bound for Calais. Numerous photos were taken with the white cliffs of Dover in the background.

Once we reached French soil, we re-boarded the bus and continued on our way through the French countryside until we arrived at Joinville Le Pont for our three-night stay. After dinner, we were treated to a night tour of the Paris illuminations.

The next day was a full day to enjoy the sights of Paris. In the evening, we were given the freedom for a fast food dinner before we headed to the Latin Quarter for a cabaret show in an old theatre.

We took our seats whilst champagne was poured. It was a carnival atmosphere and the noise levels erupted when the dancing girls, wearing frilly dresses, made their way onto the stage. The performers exhibited their prowess at the cancan, which had everyone jumping.

"Hey Frank! Could you pass me over more of that champagne?" Max called out.

I shouted back. "Yes I can-can!"

Most of the group were slightly hung-over the next morning as we visited the spectacular Palace of Versailles with its breathtaking gardens. The afternoon allowed for more exploring around central Paris, which included a saunter down the avenues and lounging in the cafés and bars. After our evening meal, we had a relaxing time at camp.

It was an early morning start to pack up, leave Paris, and head through the wonderful wine region of Burgundy en route to our next stop at a chateau in the heart of the Beaujolais. We were able to slip in some wine tasting before our evening meal and we finished off at a lively disco.

The next day offered an optional excursion to see the scenery around the chateau, cycling through the picturesque local villages, and enjoying a typical French-fare picnic lunch. It was a glorious day and the select picnic spot was on the hill referred to as the 'Top of the World'.

We were on the move again the following day, heading south with a stop at the majestic Roman aqueduct, Pont du Gard.

We progressed through France into Spain, and arrived at our campsite in Barcelona. The camp was well equipped, with a games room, bar, swimming pools, and a water slide. It was located some way out of central Barcelona, so we had a local dinner and spent the evening enjoying the camp facilities.

Early morning and Barcelona beckoned. We were driven to the Gothic Quarter of the port city. It was a sunny day and we paraded up and down La Rambla. We then walked to Gaudí's cathedral, La Sagrada Familia.

I was stunned by the artwork. "To think it was commenced over 100 years ago," I said with awe.

"I believe they still plan to have it finished," Max remarked.

"Not that it matters," I said. "It's already a masterpiece."

After a panoramic view from Mont-Juic, we returned to camp to prepare for the evening, which was supposed to be a night of Spanish cuisine, music, and dancing.

The restaurant was a cellar-style cantina with a small stage that jutted from one of the side walls. The seating consisted of rows of benches placed either side of long wooden tables.

I joined the two couples, as well as Susannah, Sally, Val, Max, James, and Shane. Shane was a happy chappy who loved his booze, and as I didn't mind a drink either, we enthusiastically pursued our common interest. To our delight, the tables were lined with carafes of sangria.

We were served a typical Spanish meal, including gazpacho, tapas, and a huge paella to share. We were entertained with Spanish music, which highlighted flamenco dancing and singing.

"This flamenco singing is really sung with feeling," commented Sally.

"Yes, it is sung with feeling," I agreed, "and I think that feeling is pain."

The night seemed to go on and on. Martin pointed out that Lanky had to drive into France tomorrow and that we should leave earlier rather than later. As we were leaving, we noticed a professional photographer taking photos of tourists wearing a montero.

The bullfighting hat was slapped on my head as I sat in a drunken stupor. I poked out my tongue as a photograph was taken. Inspection of the photograph drew many laughs, as I looked more like a member of the Mouseketeers than a bullfighter.

"Do you take this photograph?" asked the photographer.

I responded, "I do."

The next day, we headed back to France through Antibes and stopped off to check out a Mediterranean beach before travelling the additional short distance to our campsite.

The following morning, we drove along the Cote d'Azur, where we stopped to visit a perfumery and had a stroll around the promenades and marinas. We returned to camp for dinner, before venturing into the principality of Monaco, where we viewed the royal palace and visited the casino.

Italy was the next country on the itinerary, and the bus headed south to the charming ancient city of Pisa with its beautiful Romanesque architecture.

I joined Max and James in a race up the stairs to the top of the leaning tower, where we enjoyed the panoramic views.

The tour moved on to Florence, where the accommodation was in a villa with magnificent views of the beautiful Renaissance city. We dined at the villa and then headed into town to check out a local disco.

The following day was a full day in Florence, with the highlight expected to be Michelangelo's sculpture of David. We were initially taken to a leather factory before we wandered through central Florence to admire the many attractions and sights. We had an exceptionally knowledgeable guide, who walked us through the Duomo and provided an excellent historical, artistic, and engineering account of the works.

The guide then gave us some unexpected news. "We will not be able to view the statue of David due the closure of the Galleria dell'Accademia as a result of a workers' strike. Nevertheless, we will take you to the Piazza della Signoria, which is where the replica of the statue is on display, which was its original location. So at least you can witness the replica of the statue in its originally designated place."

"At least that's something," James remarked with a shrug.

"But it's not the original," I said. "It's not the same."

We returned to the villa and dressed for a meal out on the town. The dinner was at a *casa rustica*, which served homestyle Italian cooking. The diners comprised a broad mix of people from various countries. It was a lively atmosphere, with our group being placed on a few benches. The food was basic but very good, and there was a plentiful quantity of beer and wine consumed.

Max, James, and I were socialising with a group of young American women. I soon found myself outside chatting with Karen from Florida, who was studying at a university in Florence. She was an attractive lady in her mid-twenties, with brown eyes, blonde-brown hair, full lips, and a curvaceous body.

"So, what do you think about coming back to my place tonight?" Karen suggested.

"I'm not sure. I'd certainly like to, but we're leaving for Rome early tomorrow morning," I said as casually as I could in my effort to conceal my true feeling of incredulity at having been made the offer.

"Tomorrow morning is a long time away, and where's your sense of adventure?" Karen queried, running her fingers along my arm.

I was in an unprecedented quandary, still unbelieving that she was genuine in her invitation and suspecting there was something else at play. Nonetheless, I eventually threw caution to the wind and headed off with her.

"Over here, Frank; we'll catch a bus," Karen instructed.

The moment I made it to the bus stop, Karen's tongue was down my throat and we commenced a tongue wrestle. I felt awkward, as I was conscious of a multitude of people lined up at the bus stop, some of whom were looking in our direction. I was saved by the arrival of the bus.

"Where can I purchase a ticket?" I asked Karen.

"I've been living in Florence for nine months and I've never purchased a bus ticket," Karen admitted.

The bus took off and, in true Italian tradition, the driver floored it. As he rounded the bends, I had to hang on to something for dear life, and that something happened to be Karen's rump. This brought a large smile to her face and we had another bout of tongue wrestling.

Before I could steady myself, Karen hit the buzzer, the bus slammed to a stop, and she dragged me off.

The minute Karen closed the door to her apartment, she jumped me. There was a mad scramble to undress as Karen guided me to her bedroom and onto the bed. It was a whirlwind of emotion and sensuality that came to its natural climax.

"Wow, Frank, it's a pity you're leaving tomorrow." Karen sighed as I rolled off her, hyperventilating.

We rested for a while and then we started to become playful again. We were building up our intensity when I heard a noise from inside the apartment.

"What's that?" I asked.

"Oh, it's probably my roommate," said Karen. "But don't worry. He's cool."

*A male roommate?* "I'd better be going as we're leaving early," I said as I collected my belongings. We exchanged details before I departed.

It was indeed an early start. The tour headed south to the eternal city of Rome, where we settled into tents. After lunch, we headed for the centre to visit

171

the Roman Forum, Circus Maximus, the Trevi Fountain, Piazza Venezia, and the Colosseum. We then made our way back to the campsite, where we freshened up before heading off for an enjoyable restaurant meal in town.

Doing my own thing the next morning, I made my way to the Vatican. I roamed St. Peter's Square, where I was highly impressed with the dimensions, angles, and symmetrical formation of the columns. I entered the basilica and took my time appreciating the various chapels, tombs, and dome before proceeding to the Sistine Chapel to marvel at the works of Michelangelo. In the afternoon, I joined the others in an expedition to the Catacombs.

On day 14 of the tour, we headed south towards Mount Vesuvius. We were on the motorway when the bus came to a sudden stop. Lanky inspected the engine and attempted to continue the journey, but the bus slowed and halted once again.

Lanky made another attempt to ascertain the cause of the problem, whilst a couple of highway policemen pulled up on their motorbikes, which gave the women something to get excited about. The police questioned Martin and Lanky, before Martin reported back to the group.

"Well, it appears we have serious mechanical problems. We will need to get someone out to take a look, which may take some time. We're also contacting the company to have a replacement bus on standby. Unfortunately, either way, we won't be able

172

to visit Pompeii."

Huge sighs of disappointment filled the bus.

The mechanic arrived, but to no avail. A tow truck was then called as we waited for a replacement bus. Four hours later, we were on our way again.

Lanky made a sterling effort to traverse the southern Italian roads to arrive at Brindisi in time for us to grab a bite to eat before boarding the ferry bound for Greece.

The port at Brindisi was busy with tourists, which heightened the atmosphere of sheer chaos and commercial exploitation. We grabbed a bite from a restaurant offering a tourist menu. We then returned to the bus to collect our luggage before boarding the *Poseidon* ferry for the crossing to Patras.

We travelled by bus along the Peloponnese coast and across the Corinth Canal to Athens, staying in a *pensione* located in Glyfada, a beach on the outer fringes of the city.

We went to a restaurant in the Plaka area, where we enjoyed traditional Greek food and music. It was a fairly early night as we prepared for the next day and our destination of the Greek island of Mykonos.

The ferry departed from the port of Piraeus. We were looking forward to the island stint as it was the halfway mark of our European adventure and it gave us the opportunity to have a relaxing base for six days.

Mykonos was a beautiful island with whitewashed houses, windmills, and boutique stores. The streets were cobbled and surrounded by pristine, sandy beaches.

Accommodation was in a comfortable hotel with a swimming pool. Max, James, and I shared a room, and we took little time in making ourselves at home. We lined the ceiling with makeshift clothes lines and, before long, our room looked like a disaster zone.

We quickly got into the island routine. We had late-morning starts, eating a light brunch while relaxing by the pool. The afternoon was the time for buggie rides, shopping, or going to the beach. This was followed by a siesta before dinner and our attack on the nightlife. It was hard to know what to look forward to the most, as each part of the day had its own rewards.

The six days on Mykonos elapsed quickly and we took the ferry back to the mainland, where we returned to the hotel at Glyfada in Athens.

The following day, we had a guided tour of Athens that took in the Acropolis, the Parthenon, and the parliament building. We travelled westward back to Patras for our return ferry ride to Brindisi. We were then driven up the east coast of Italy, arriving at our overnight stay in Casalbordino.

We proceeded through the Republic of San Marino and on to Venice, where we had twin-share accommodation on the island of Lido in a grand building that was formerly a monastery. There was an option to take a gondola ride just before sunset that included being serenaded.

I asked Sally if she would accompany me, but she was already paired off with another woman. I then asked Susannah and she agreed. The gondolier wove his craft along the waterways and serenaded part of the way. It was a pleasant ride and I was just getting comfortable when it abruptly came to an end.

Saturday was a beautiful, sunny day and we ventured via waterbus from the Lido to Piazza San Marco. We were taken to see some leatherwear and demonstrations of glass-blowing before being permitted free time. I joined several group members to view the various famous bridges and canals before we sat down at one of the many canal-side cafés and sipped on cappuccinos.

We took off the next day through the Dolomite mountain range and into Austria, where we set up at a campsite in Vienna.

The splendours of the Schönbrunn Palace and the Hofburg were the highlights of the following day, with the evening meal at a restaurant in the Vienna Woods.

Leaving Vienna, we travelled on to the fairytale city of Salzburg, which boasted fine examples of baroque-style architecture, the birthplace of Mozart, and parks containing a monument of Mozart.

We had a photo stop at the house from the movie *The Sound of Music* and then moved through to Germany, stopping at Munich, the capital of the famous beer state of Bavaria.

We visited the Deutsches Museum, St Peter's

Tower, and the Olympic Complex, stage for the 1972 Olympic Games. I was so obsessed with the Glockenspiel in the Marienplatz that I hung around for two hours to enjoy a repeat sounding. Later, we visited the Dachau Concentration Camp. We had some time to rest before we headed out for the evening.

Dinner was at a typical Bavarian beer hall. We were getting stuck into the beers when a band appeared — a form of Umpapa band. People cringed at first, but they got into the swing of things after consuming more of the amber ale.

"It's the chicken song, the chicken song," I would shout out at the start of each new song. To my surprise, as I shouted it out once more, the chicken song actually started playing.

Everyone was having a fabulous time, and even Sally, who normally didn't drink much, seemed happily intoxicated. There were only a handful of people remaining by the end of the night, with Sally and I catching a cab together.

I advised the taxi driver of our destination and relaxed into the back seat next to Sally. We initially got cosy and I was stunned when she initiated some fondling and kissing, which we engaged in for the rest of the drive.

When we arrived back at camp, we were walking back to our tents, hand in hand, when we started to become friendly again. Sally soon pulled away. "I'd better get back. Susannah may be concerned about my whereabouts."

As Sally walked off, I sat on a swing and took a moment to contemplate what could have been.

# Chapter 25

## A Near-Death Experience

The following morning, the tour left Germany through the Bavarian Alps. We re-entered Austria and stopped off for a break to go white-water rafting. We had a decent tussle with the river rapids before we were back on the bus. We travelled through Innsbruck to the gorgeous village of Hopfgarten and our accommodation at a delightful *gasthof*.

After the heavy night before and a long, tiring day, we appreciated a relaxing evening, with dinner at the *gasthof*. This was followed by quiet drinks at the bar. At least, that's the way it started.

Glen, Shane, and I got socialising with the barman, and the discussion found its way to the topic of the schnapps challenge. It was described as an informal tradition where the guests would see who could down the greatest number of schnapps shots. The record for one night was claimed to be 51 shots, held by an American female.

"I'm up for the challenge," Shane declared.

"So am I," Glen exclaimed.

I wasn't really interested; however, in the spirit of the schnapps tradition, I stated, "I'll drink to that!"

Shane commenced the proceedings. "So what do we have here, bartender?"

"We have a reasonable selection of a variety of schnapps flavours," the bartender explained.

"How many flavours exactly?" Glen asked, and the barman pointed to a list.

"Well, we'll have to try them all," Shane decreed.

"Why don't we take it from the top, so it makes it easier to keep track of what we've had?" Glen suggested.

"What a great way to start, with apple," Shane said.

"I really like the banana one," commented Glen.

"I prefer the apricot," Shane said. "And this butterscotch is out of this world."

"I don't know about the chocolate one," I said.

"Hey Glen, the next one's kiwi; it will give me great pleasure downing this one," Shane said.

"Spearmint? Haven't we had the spearmint?" Glen asked.

"No, that was the peppermint," I replied.

I felt heavily intoxicated and indicated that I might call it quits.

"Come on, Frank," Shane urged. "You can't desert us now."

"What's this Stroh thing?" Glen interrupted.

"Yeah, bartender, what's Stroh?" Shane pried further.

"Stroh Obstschnapps is a natural and fruity schnapps that has been handed down through generations of the Stroh family," the bartender explained.

"Okay then. We'll have to drink it in honour of the Stroh family," I proposed. "To the Stroh family!"

"To the Stroh family!" came the universal reply.

"Hey, bartender, what about that Stroh rum?" Glen queried as he took hold of the bottle and started reading aloud. "STROH Original is the best aromatic expression of the Austrian way of life." He then decreed, "We'll have to taste the aromatic expression of the Austrian way of life!"

"It's also, technically, on the schnapps list," Shane added.

Glen and Shane then looked over to me and there was a moment of silence as they waited for my reply. "What the hell," I declared. "I'll drink to that!"

I was the first to belt down the Stroh rum. "Bloody hell," I cried in disgust. "This is bloomin' rocket fuel!"

"All right!" Shane cheered, and he also knocked back a Stroh rum. "Yikes. You're not kidding. This stuff's lethal."

"What's this big number 80 on the front of the bottle?" Glen queried.

"That's 80% alcohol by volume," replied the bartender.

"Holy shit!" Glen blasphemed as he downed his shot.

"Well, I think that should do," suggested the bartender.

"You've got to be joking," I stated. "I can't go to

bed with this rough taste in my mouth. Now, which was the schnapps I liked the most?"

In the morning, my roommates woke me.

"Could you keep it down please, fellas," I pleaded.

"Come on, Frank. Get up," encouraged James.

"Leave me alone," I grumbled. "I feel horrible."

"Today will be our only chance to explore the village, so if you want to join us cycling into town, best you get up," Max explained.

Complaining, I crawled out of bed and got dressed.

"You can hire the bicycles from over there," James said, pointing.

"I don't even have any money," I mumbled.

"That's okay. I'll pay for you," Sally said.

"Thanks Sally. I'll pay you back later," I said, mounting a bike.

"Oi, Frank, you're going the wrong way!" Max shouted.

I completed a U-turn and headed back towards the others. I was still under the influence of alcohol, tired, and dehydrated. Riding on the wrong side of the road for Europe, I followed the road around the bend and sought to mount the footpath, but there was a road barrier. I looked up, and a car was coming straight for me.

\*   \*   \*

My sight was blurry, but I could make out the

181

vision of a beautiful young blonde. I couldn't discern who she was or how far away she was, but I tried to reach for her.

The woman initially tried to veer away, but as she noticed me continuing to reach for her, she took my arm and placed it under the blankets.

*A nurse, and I'm in hospital,* I realised. *The car must have collected me.*

As my vision cleared, I noticed a number of tubes inserted into various parts of my anatomy. One was up a nostril, there were a couple coming out of my arm, one emanating from my belly, and, upon lifting the blankets, I saw another hanging off my willy.

The nurse left me alone in the room and I wondered about my condition.

The nurse soon returned with a doctor in tow. "Hello. How are you feeling?" the doctor asked.

"Oh, I'm feeling fine, thanks Doctor."

"You had quite a collision."

"Yes, I guess I came off second best. Was anyone else hurt?"

"Apart from some very concerned people, you were the only one who sustained any physical injuries," the doctor said. "Fortunately, the worst is over, but we still have a few things we need to attend to. We will leave you to your dinner and provide you with a proper diagnosis tomorrow morning. How does that sound?"

"That sounds fine. Thanks Doctor."

The next morning, an attractive young nurse

named Jane entered the room. "Good morning Frank."

"Good morning Jane."

"Did you enjoy your breakfast?"

"It was great thanks. The food in this hospital is very good."

"The doctor should be here in an hour or so. Did you want to have your sponge bath before he arrives?"

"I think the doctor would appreciate that," I said. "Will you be giving me the bath today, Jane?"

"No, Frank. You know we have special staff for that."

"Oh yeah, that's right. The older female staff who train in Greco-Roman wrestling."

After my bath, the doctor entered the room. "Good morning Frank. I will provide your diagnosis now," he advised. "You had a fairly solid impact and when you arrived at the hospital you were critical. However, after we operated, we were able to stabilise your condition. You were in shock. In fact, you may still have some mild shock and it may take a little more time for you to get over it. Our greatest concern was your spleen, which had ruptured, so we removed it. You also have a bruised left kidney, a series of broken ribs on your left side, a fracture of your left shoulder blade, and a temporary skull fracture, also on the left-hand side. That's basically it. So do you have any questions?"

"What do you mean by a temporary skull

fracture?" I asked.

"It is a hairline fracture that will mend itself over time," the doctor explained.

"What about the other fractures and broken ribs?"

"They should also heal naturally, over time. You should be well enough to commence mobilisation in a day or two and after a week we can commence further movement, physiotherapy, and exercise. How does that sound, Frank?"

"Sounds good, Doctor," I said, trying to take it all in.

The doctor left and, soon after, a nurse entered. "Excuse me, Frank, you have a telephone call; it's your parents."

"Oh no. Do they know about the accident?"

"I'm afraid they do and they seem very concerned."

I picked up the handset. "Hello."

"Hello. Frank, how are you?" Joe asked in his usual, strong voice.

"I'm fine, Dad. Everything is fine."

"How can you be fine? From what the hospital told us, we thought you were going to die!"

"I had a bit of an accident, that's all. They're taking really good care of me and I'll be okay."

"Hang on, Frank. Your mother wants to hear your voice."

"Hello Frank," Mary said, crying.

"Hi Mum. I'm fine. There's no need to cry."

Mary continued to sob as Joe took back the

184

phone. "Frank."

"Yes, Dad?"

"Do we need to send someone to bring you home?"

"Dad, that's not necessary, believe me. I'm well and getting better. I'll be perfectly all right, and when I leave here, I'll be visiting our relatives. They're bound to take good care of me."

"Hmm. All right, but if you need anything, you call us," Joe instructed.

"No problem, Dad. The people here in Austria are fantastic and they're taking really good care of me. In fact, another patient told me I was lucky to have had my accident here, rather than in Italy. Apparently the hospitals here in the Austrian Tyrolean mountains are amongst the best, while the hospital care in Italy is said to be rubbish."

"Now, that I can believe," Joe said.

Later that day, a young man visited me. "Hello Frank. My name is Josh and I work for the tour company. I hope you're feeling better?"

"Hello Josh. I'm feeling much better, thanks."

"I was asked to let you know that we have organised everything with your insurance company. They have confirmed your cover and are dealing directly with the hospital to pay your bills. The only cost they won't cover is this charge from the police," Josh explained.

"The police?" I queried. "What do they charge for?"

"I understand it's a traffic fine," Josh replied. "Apparently, whenever there's an accident someone has to pay a fine and, in this case, you're the one. Anyway, there are a bunch of guys you might know who would like to speak to you. I'll telephone them for you now ... Here you go, Frank."

"Hello?" I said.

"Howdy, Frank; it's Martin."

"Hi Martin. How's everything going?"

"Things are going well, but more to the point, how are you?"

"I'm fine. How's the tour going?"

"It's been good, but there's a bunch of people that miss you. Hang on ..."

"Frankie! G'day mate."

"Shane! G'day to you too. I hope you've been making up for the booze I've missed out on."

"No fear about that, Frank."

"Hello Duckie."

"Max, you idiot, how's it going, mate?"

"I'm fine, but I'm really sorry I left you in Hopfgarten."

"Sorry? What for? I was the dunce who played chicken with a car. You just make sure you enjoy yourself for the both of us."

"Hi Frank."

"Sally, hi. I'm really sorry, Sally; I owe you the money from the bike hire."

"Frank, you're unbelievable. Don't worry about that. I just wish you were here."

"So do I, Sally."

"It's Martin again. Susannah and James, as well as all the rest of the gang, say hi and wish you all the best. As you know, everyone was signing and adding things to our tour book and they unanimously voted to send it to you. We also have a T-shirt everyone has signed. We'll send you that as well."

"Gee," I said, "I'm really touched."

"Is that all you've got to say, Duckie?" Max said.

"Well, I was also thinking about the things a guy has to go through just to get a free T-shirt."

\*   \*   \*

I had been in hospital for almost two weeks and had improved markedly. "When might I be able to leave?" I asked the doctor.

"Given your progress with the physiotherapy, and your improved condition, you may leave whenever you want," the doctor replied.

*Whenever I want*, I wondered. *It seems odd that the decision to leave is left up to me.* "Okay, what about if I leave the day after tomorrow."

"The day after tomorrow," repeated the doctor. "I shall commence arrangements to see whether we can discharge you on Saturday morning, the third of September. We shall let you know tomorrow morning, Frank."

"Thank you, Doctor."

The next morning, the doctor visited me with a

nurse and a physiotherapist. "Good morning Frank. We have good news. Your discharge for tomorrow has been approved; however, it is subject to conditions. Firstly, discharge is on the basis that you are released to home care, which means you are required to stay with someone for a further week."

"But I don't know anyone with whom I can stay."

"That's fine," the doctor said. "The tour company has made enquiries and there is a family that has a farm near the *gasthof* where you can stay if you are agreeable."

"That's great. Of course I'm agreeable."

"Good, then. The only additional things you need to know are the physiotherapy exercises, which the physiotherapist will go over with you, and the medication you will need to take, which will be administered by the nurse. Well, Frank, that's it. I wish you all the best."

"Thank you, Doctor; you saved my life."

The doctor smiled. "No problem. I was just doing my job."

It was Saturday morning and the time for my discharge. I gathered my things and thanked the staff who'd taken care of me.

"The taxi is waiting outside for you, Frank," Jane advised.

"Thank you, Jane. Goodbye."

"Goodbye Frank."

The taxi took me by a timber yard and I immediately recalled the familiar scent of pine. It was the same scent I'd smelt on that fateful day. The taxi arrived at the farm and made its way up the drive to where a woman, a man, a girl, and a boy waited to greet me.

"Hello. It is Frank, *ja*?" said the woman.

"Yes, I am Frank."

"This is my husband, Marcus, my daughter, Isabelle, my son, Helmut, and I am Ingrid."

"Hello everyone."

"Wait," Ingrid said. "Marcus will take your bags; it must be difficult for you with that sling."

"Thank you, Ingrid and Marcus."

"We will show you to your room. You can settle in and we can then have some lunch," Ingrid said.

"That sounds wonderful," I replied.

After settling into my room, I descended the timber staircase to the kitchen. "Is everything in order, Frank?" asked Ingrid.

"Yes, thank you, Ingrid. This is a lovely home; I like it very much."

"Children, lunch is ready! Marcus is tending to the cows, but he should be back shortly. You may sit here, Frank, at the head of the table. Marcus is at the other end. The children will sit on that side and I will sit on this side," Ingrid instructed.

Marcus returned and took his seat at the table, which was the cue for dinner to be served.

"Excuse me, Mother, is it all right if Helmut and I take Frank for a walk to the village?" Isabelle asked.

"That is a nice thought, but Frank may not yet be

ready to go to the village," Ingrid said. "You can take him another time, if he wishes."

"Thank you, Isabelle," I stated. "Your mother is right. I don't feel strong enough to go to the village; however, I would like to go for a walk around the farm after lunch, if that's all right."

"Yes, Mother, we can show Frank the farm!" Helmut said with an exuberance not usually allowed at the dinner table, which he seemed to realise as the words passed his lips. "Sorry, Mother."

"That's all right, Helmut," Ingrid said. "I think that would be good."

"Thank you, Ingrid. Lunch was delicious," I said.

"I'm glad you liked it. Now, children, you may take Frank for a walk."

Marcus immediately followed. "I can show you a few things around the farm," he said, with a hint of pride in his voice.

"That would be great, thanks Marcus. I really like farms."

The children burst out of the house, ran around with what seemed to be limitless energy, and began playing with their two dogs. The dogs then paid their respects to the stranger by approaching me, sniffing around, and wagging their tails.

"Hello, you guys," I said as I patted the dogs alternately with my right hand, as I had my left arm in the sling.

"Children, take the dogs and lead the way," directed Marcus, and the children happily obeyed.

"We have a few hectares of land where we run dairy cows and some sheep. It is not a huge commercial concern, but we make a little money, as we do with renting some rooms. I retired from an engineering job and I thought I would pursue my love of farming. Ingrid is happy and the children seem to enjoy it," Marcus modestly explained.

"Yes, your children definitely seem happy, and this scenery is beautiful," I said as I took in the rolling green hills.

"Yes, it is," agreed Marcus with contentment. "Let me know when you are ready to return to the house."

Marcus showed me his animals, the sheds, and pointed out the extent of his land. I waited until I sensed that he had shown me the main attractions. "I think I might be ready to return," I advised.

"Children, we are heading back now," Marcus shouted.

I settled in well with the family, largely due to the fact that they were perfect hosts. Ingrid was the most sociable, and Marcus was friendly, though more reserved. The children were quiet and respectful in the common areas of the house, but opened up into happy, playful children outdoors. I concluded that it must be due to a good upbringing. I thoroughly enjoyed my time with the family and the walks with the children to the village were a highlight.

After six days at the farmhouse, I felt that I was just about strong enough to move on. I took the opportunity to visit the *gasthof* and found Josh. "Hi

Josh, I'm about to set off now. I really want to thank you, Martin, Lanky, and the tour company for everything you've done for me. I really appreciate it."

"It was no problem, Frank. I was going to come over to the farmhouse to give you these small items. You may already know what they are," Josh said, handing me a package.

"Yes, I think I do. Thanks Josh."

I returned to the farmhouse to thank and say goodbye to the family.

The taxi made its way through to Hopfgarten's neighbouring town of Worgl and dropped me off at the train station. My first rail journey was from Worgl to Innsbruck, with a connecting train from Innsbruck to Lucerne.

Checking into my accommodation in central Lucerne, I rested and was contemplating the incidences of the last month, with many thoughts entering my mind.

*Did I leave Hopfgarten too early? I'm still thin and feel weak. I've never met my Italian relatives before. It will be awkward to meet them for the first time, especially in my condition. What a pity the accident occurred, as it caused me to miss out on the last week of the tour.*

# Chapter 26

## Meeting the Relatives

I found Lucerne to be a perfect stopover to convalesce. The town was situated on the northwest extremity of the Lake of Lucerne, with the Reuss River flowing through it.

The old town featured the original gate, the town wall, watchtowers, and cobbled streets. I was impressed by the distinctive architecture of the city and the Chapel Bridge with its water tower. I was also moved by the Lion of Lucerne, a sculpture carved in 1821 out of solid rock, being a monument to the Swiss Guards who were slaughtered defending Paris in 1792 during the French Revolution.

The train ride from Lucerne Station to Genoa took just over six hours. I then needed to ring my relatives. My Italian was limited and my nerves took hold. My movements were almost in slow motion as I subconsciously delayed the inevitable.

"Where are those silly *gettoni*?" I complained as I searched for the Italian phone tokens. I made the call and spoke to Alba, one of my mother's cousins. We went through some preliminary introductions and then she instructed me to take the No. 18 bus.

Catching the bus, I asked the driver to notify me of my stop. I was relieved to find him much more restrained than the bus driver I had experienced in Florence. Once alerted of the stop, I alighted the vehicle and climbed the hill.

Locating the address, I rang the bell and spoke to Alba via the intercom. She arranged for another of my mother's cousins, Nina, to escort me up to the apartment via a small, rickety elevator that we had to squeeze into. The front door was open when we arrived at the top floor and I was shown into an apartment with views towards central Genoa.

After introductions to Mary's other cousins and their two teenage children, I settled in and freshened up before dinner. They were all fussing over me and I didn't mind it in the least.

Dinner was served on the balcony — the usual practice during summer. It was a plentiful and scrumptious meal, which we rounded off with percolated coffee and homemade limoncello.

During my stay in Genoa, my relatives escorted me to many attractions, including the port area and the Italian Riviera. It was a beautiful and proud city that highlighted the contribution of its most famous former citizen: Christopher Columbus. I had a happy time during my stay in Genoa and my relatives were disappointed at the news of my leaving.

The relatives left early on the day of my departure and I spent the day seeing to my final preparations. Mid-afternoon, I made my way out of the apartment block, via the rickety elevator, walked down the hill, and caught the bus to Genoa Station.

I took the overnight train to the city of Bari on the Adriatic coast in southern Italy. The train arrived at six o'clock in the morning and I was then required to take another small train to the country town of Mary's birthplace.

Arriving at midday, I found a public phone booth and made the call. My aunt, Clara, lived close by and I made my way along narrow streets before knocking on the door of a small, old brick house.

There was an excited welcome as I was invited in and introduced to my grandmother, Maria, who cried at the sight of me, as I resembled my mother in some ways.

As emotions calmed, spirits lifted, and happiness took over. We discussed many things and, as the day progressed, more and more of my relatives arrived.

After having stayed only a few days, my departure dampened the happy mood. I was escorted to the train station, where my relatives waved me farewell as the train pulled away.

I took the train from Bari to Foggia, then a bus up the mountain range to my father's birthplace.

It was overcast and gloomy when the creaky old bus reached the mountains. I was exhausted, with my arm and ribs causing me pain, as the bus tugged up the mountains and slowly weaved its way through the valleys.

On arrival, I was again in search of a public phone

and made yet another call. Again, it was fortuitous the house was very close. I walked the narrow, cobbled streets and quickly found the address. In a flash, Angela opened the door and greeted me. I was then introduced to Rita, who took my bags and sat me down.

Joe had scant surviving relatives, comprising a few cousins and their families. Rita was Joe's cousin and Angela was her daughter. They chatted with me for a little while before they led me to a room that they had set aside for me. They gave me time to settle in before dinner.

I was introduced to Rita's husband, Antonio, and their son, Vito. We had an enjoyable dinner and I was made to feel at home. The relatives sensed that I was tired and encouraged me to get some rest.

In the morning, I was feeling much better and Angela took me to the town centre, where a crowd had gathered. Joe was a popular character, and even though he had left the town some forty years earlier, the townsfolk remembered or had heard of him and were enthusiastic to meet his son.

Many of the townsfolk shook my hand. A booming voice then echoed from the midst of the crowd and a solid old man approached and hugged me. The man soon introduced himself as Pepe, a close friend of Joe's. Pepe insisted on taking me on a tour of the town to check out some of Joe's old haunts.

In every place we entered, whether it was a café, a

bar, or a shop, there were people who knew or had heard about Joe, which made me feel tremendously proud.

I spent the next few days visiting Joe's family and friends. Every meeting was a grand affair and an eating extravaganza. I enjoyed the continued tradition of the *passeggiata*, where the townsfolk socialised during their daily promenade along the streets after dinner.

The news of my impending departure was met with sadness and many of the townsfolk gathered to see me off.

My return bus trip through the mountains was not the overcast and gloomy experience of my arrival. The sun was breaking through, I felt uplifted, and I was eager to hear my parents' voices again.

Arriving at Foggia, I was checking the timetable for Rome when I came across the one for Naples. *Naples! That's near Pompeii and not far from here. It's closer than Rome. In fact, it's virtually on the way to Rome, in a roundabout way. Why didn't I ever think of this before? It's perfect.*

Regretting having missed out on Pompeii on the European tour, I purchased a ticket for Naples.

The train eventually arrived in Naples and I couldn't wait to call my parents. I rushed to the telephones at the station and dialled the number. The phone rang and rang and then rang out. *Why don't they answer? What day is it? It's Saturday here, so it's Sunday morning there. Dad must have taken Mum to church.*

I found hotel accommodation and, after I had checked in, I tried to ring my parents again. The phone rang for some time and I started to worry. *It's almost 10.00 p.m. here, which would make it around midday there. They should be home now.* Just as I was expecting the phone to ring out again, Mary answered.

"Hello, Ma!"

"Frank, how are you?"

"I'm fine, Ma. How are you?"

"I am good."

"I've met your family, Ma, and they all send you their love," I said excitedly.

"That's good," she whispered, and I could hear her fighting back tears.

"Who is it?" Joe's voice sounded in the background.

"It's Frank."

"What's wrong now?"

"There's nothing wrong. He met the family. Here. Talk to him."

"Hey."

"Hi, Pa. I met your family and friends. They all say hello and send you their love. I had no idea how many friends you have and how popular you are," I said with admiration.

"Ah yeah. I know," was Joe's matter-of-fact reaction.

"Anyway, I'm in Naples now and I'm going to visit Pompeii," I declared.

"Oh, Naples," Joe stated. "I remember Naples

from when I was in the navy."

I thought I'd better interrupt, just in case he was going to recite one of his never-ending monologues. "Hey, Pa?"

"What, son?"

"I love you, Pa."

Joe was not one to show emotion. "Yeah, yeah. You just take care of yourself and come home safely."

"Okay, Pa. Can I speak to Mum again?"

"Here. Your son wants to speak to you."

"Yes, Frank?"

"I love you, Ma."

"I love you too, son."

*     *     *

I booked a tour of Pompeii and the Amalfi Coast for the following day. Then I used the remainder of the day to enjoy some of the attractions in Naples.

The tour bus the next morning was only half full with about a dozen, mainly middle-aged, travellers. When we arrived at Pompeii, we were escorted through the site by a guide.

I was overcome with an eerie feeling as I walked along the excavated streets and looked into the rooms, buildings, and areas with the various exhibits and archaeological finds. I viewed the exhibits in the museum erected near the Porta Marina, one of the eight gates of the city. I strolled down the streets, including Via dell' Abbondanza that once contained an amphitheatre and several houses. I had to take a few backstreets to track down the popular attraction of Lupanare, the once-famed brothel of Pompeii, where phalluses engraved on the rocks of roads and the stones of buildings pointed the way to its location.

We left Pompeii around midday and drove along the Amalfi Coast, where we stopped at a café for a spot of lunch. Continuing along the coast, we were treated to views out to the Gulf of Naples and the Gulf of Salerno. We also enjoyed views of the towns of Sorrento, Amalfi, and the place of the rich and famous: Positano.

Returning to Naples, I had a small dinner, walked around the local streets near the railway station, and then retired to my hotel room.

Taking the first train to Rome, I arrived around midday. Even though I'd had a hearty breakfast I was still hungry, so I had a snack at the railway station before finding a reasonable hotel at a modest rate.

I wanted a few days to rest before my first flight after my traffic accident. My condition had improved, though I was still weak and was getting headaches. With two weeks of my travels remaining, I decided to split the time equally between Rome and London.

I took it easy during my time in Rome and I felt good as I caught the plane to London. I was grateful it was a smooth flight, and I settled into a bed and breakfast.

Each day, armed with my camera and my list of attractions, I paced myself to travel the length and breadth of central London. From Kensington Palace to Buckingham Palace; from Big Ben to the Tower of London; I ticked off the numerous attractions from my list as I went along. I was ecstatic that I managed to see all the sights I had hoped to visit.

It was Tuesday morning on 18 October 1988 when I left London and caught my Singapore Airlines flight bound for Melbourne.

Flying into Tullamarine Airport on Thursday morning, I gazed over Australia's wide-open spaces. It was a smooth passage through immigration and I was unfazed at having to wait for my luggage. I was cleared through customs and, as the automatic sliding doors opened, I was preparing to make a turn for the taxi rank when my parents came into view.

We hurried towards each other and hugged. Mary was crying and even Joe, who often boasted he had never shed a tear in his life, was slightly emotional.

"Come on. Let's hurry up and go home!" Joe stated in an authoritative voice.

"Yeah," I said. "Let's go home."

# Chapter 27

## Back to Work

I returned to Australia on Thursday, 20 October 1988 and spent the afternoon unpacking. I was changing my clothes when I noticed my topless body in the mirror. With all the excitement of my travels, I had not previously noted the visible signs of my injuries.

I looked to where I once had distinctive abdominal muscle definition, but my six-pack had vanished. In its place was a deep red scar that extended from just under my left nipple, zigzagged diagonally down, bypassing my belly button, and ended above my right hip.

I had been warned that my inactivity in hospital and limited movement afterwards would lead to muscle atrophy, whereby I could lose as much as 1% of muscle mass per day. It had been two months since my traffic accident and my body appeared skeletal in parts, with sagging skin elsewhere.

For a few moments, I was stupefied by the sight of my ugly figure. It then dawned on me that the abdominal scar was yet another physical feature I would be self-conscious and ashamed of for the rest of my life.

After a few moments of reflection, I then had what I sensed was a landmark thought: *I guess we are all brought into the world with a unique body with distinguishing features; however, life experiences can change things for the worse. Maybe our original condition when we enter the world is not a cross we have to bear for our whole life. Maybe it's okay to change things for the better.*

I spent Friday moping around the house before I motivated myself on the weekend to look for a new car. It didn't take me too long to decide on a 1988 red MG convertible.

I returned to work on Monday, where I learned the Audit Office had undergone a revamp of positions, with the Clerical Administrative positions being restructured under Administrative Service Officer Levels (ASOL). There was much ridicule over the changed names, as many staff referred to the ASOL positions as arsehole positions. It wasn't too long before the Audit Office dropped the 'L'.

My position was essentially transferred across to an Auditor, ASO 5, without any practical change.

If I had any hopes that matters may have improved at work while I was away, they were completely dashed. All the pre-existing problems plaguing the Audit Office were exacerbated, and additional problems arose.

The Committee of Public Accounts completed its enquiry into the Audit Office in March 1989, with the main proposal being that the original *Audit Act* be replaced by two new Acts — a *Finance Act* and a new *Audit Act*. The stated effect of the new acts was to enable a modernisation of the regulatory framework and a separation from the traditional auditing requirements.

In essence, the proposal simply recommended for Australia to adopt the so-called 'best practices' of the national audit institutions of Canada, the United Kingdom, and New Zealand.

The Audit Office was experiencing a number of challenges, including the difficulty in recruiting new staff, whilst trying to implement the Committee of Public Accounts' proposal. In order to address this dilemma, a selection of financial statement audits were contracted out, despite concerns over the effect this would have on Audit Office staff motivation and morale.

As a consequence of the proposed new legislation and audit practices, it was no surprise that the Audit Office had high resignation rates and, in order to meet the staff problems, temporary contract staff were engaged through several professional recruitment agencies. A takeover of the Audit Office by external auditors seemed to have begun.

The reduced financial resources and staff available for the Audit Office were reflected during the 1989—1990 financial year, when the Melbourne regional office consolidated their accommodation from two floors to one, being the 7th floor at 303 Collins Street, Melbourne.

I thought it was most ironic that in the year when the Melbourne Office last had an accommodation change, Jessica had given birth to a child, and now, in 1990, she announced that she was expecting another child. Later that year, she gave birth to a healthy girl who was named Rose.

At the end of 1990, Heston visited me with his girlfriend, Liliana, which I was thrilled about as I had not seen too much of him in recent years. They were uncharacteristically subdued during their visit, until they divulged their true reason for calling on me.

"We're getting married!" Liliana eventually blurted out, which liberated us from the formalities.

I was genuinely elated for both of them, as I thought they were a wonderful pairing. It also made me reflect on whether I would ever find a suitable partner.

"By the way," Heston added. "We'd like you to be part of our wedding party."

I was delighted to attend as, just like at Jessica's wedding, I enjoyed VIP treatment, and, with the aid of copious amounts of alcohol, I was relaxed and had a marvellous time.

* * *

Heston returned to work after his honeymoon and it wasn't long before he contacted me to meet him for drinks after work on a Friday. We met at one of our former haunts and comfortably settled in.

I was keen to hear about his holiday, but Heston only afforded limited attention to it, as he had other things on his mind, namely the Tax Office. It seemed as though, after having had a ball on his honeymoon and upon returning to his mundane public service job, his mind was illuminated on the unpleasant situation at work.

Like most of the qualified staff in the Tax Office, Heston had achieved a rapid rise in the ranks in the early years of his career, where he was promoted from a Clerk Class 2/3 to a Clerk Class 4 in 1984, a Clerk Class 5 in 1985, and a Clerk Class 6 in 1986. However, thereafter, most Tax Office staff hit the wall. Promotion to higher levels was generally reserved for favoured staff and lackeys who cruised through a management stream, and some of them were not even qualified.

I could sympathise with Heston, as every problem he raised with the Tax Office seemed to be mirrored in the Audit Office. After we had confided in each other, rather than making us feel better, we were both miserable. By comparing our respective jobs, we realised that our exceptionally bad situations were not confined to our respective employment, but that the problems were more widespread, which left us in despair. All we could do was sulk in our beers.

*　　*　　*

I continued with my duties in a section that resembled most of the others, where the personnel reflected generational differences between the older, senior staff and the younger, newer entrants.

Most of the older staff occupied the senior positions. These senior staff also generally considered continuing professional development as unnecessary, since they bathed in the luxury of limiting themselves to management and administrative matters.

Not only was I not supported in my postgraduate courses, but I actually seemed to be resented for pursuing them.

"Who are you trying to impress with these unnecessary studies?" one senior auditor commented.

"It's not as if it's going to make you smart," another senior auditor said. "You'll just be the same old smart arse."

In response to the criticisms, I simply put my head down and concentrated on my work. Even though my section took advantage of my efforts, they did not show any appreciation for them.

On the other hand, my hard work and productivity did come to the attention of other section leaders. When one of them required the services of a senior auditor on an acting basis, I was the first to be invited to put in an expression of interest.

I was ecstatic when I was successful in attaining the acting position. I acknowledged that it was a great opportunity for me and I wanted to show my gratitude through even greater efforts.

During the period of my acting, my section leader was Mr Fairley. He was in his thirties and I considered him to be one of the more professional managers, being firm but fair. I got on very well with him, and when my 12-month acting period expired, he was quick to secure my services once again.

I had been acting in the Senior Auditor, ASO 6 position for over three years when it was advertised on a permanent basis. However, when I read the members of the selection committee, I didn't bother applying.

The committee was made up of a union representative, a management stooge, and, as Chairman, Mr Meaney.

As soon as Mr Fairley and the other managers learned I hadn't applied, they were quick to approach me.

"Why haven't you applied? None of the other applicants have your qualifications and the proven ability to undertake the work at that level," one of the managers pointed out. "It would be a shame if you didn't apply."

"I've had the privilege of being your manager for the past few years and you have consistently performed at a high level," Mr Fairley said. "If anyone should apply, it's you."

In the end I did apply, but even though I was shortlisted for an interview, somehow I had a foreboding it would be a waste of time.

The interview was more like an interrogation as Mr

Meaney challenged every single point I had made in my application to support my claims for the position. During the course of the interview, I sensed that the main reason I was shortlisted was for Mr Meaney to have the opportunity to ridicule me.

Low and behold, when the successful applicant was notified, it happened to be a member of my usual section who was a close friend and drinking mate of Mr Meaney.

I was philosophical about my unsuccessful application. It was the first time I had ever applied for a promotion in the Audit Office and I vowed it would be the last. I then smiled as I reflected. *I don't know why I bother to pursue postgraduate studies and continuous professional development when I'd have a better chance of promotion if I just went to the pub to drink with the plebs.*

The moment the result of the selection process was published, the other section leaders were quick to approach me once again. "This is an injustice; you simply must appeal."

I didn't approve of the appeals system and I certainly didn't want to be part of yet another kangaroo court in the form of an unmeritorious process through an unequal-opportunity employer.

# Chapter 28

## Medical Attention

Since returning from overseas, I was often falling ill to a series of viruses and infections. I contracted an ear infection, which I persevered with for a couple of weeks before the pain and difficulty in hearing caused me to visit my doctor.

The doctor looked into both my ears through an otoscope and referred me to an otolaryngologist. The specialist was quick with his examination, diagnosing a severe ear infection, and he placed me on antibiotics for a month.

My condition improved only marginally and the specialist extended my prescription for another month. I hoped it would be third time lucky as I visited the specialist once again.

"I don't like to prescribe antibiotics for too long," the specialist said. "But you've got a fairly virulent infection and I think it's best we get on top of it, so I'll prescribe antibiotics for one more month."

After the additional month of antibiotics, I was still feeling some sensitivity and discomfort, but I was glad to be off the daily pill-popping.

I had ongoing complications with my health and

struggled to get motivated at work, with morale in the Audit Office ever worsening. As I had often found refuge in my studies while at school, I turned to study again when, in 1990, I commenced a program for professional accountants.

I had established a routine whereby I lost myself in my work in the Audit Office and my studies. I hardly ever went out, and as soon as I had completed my accounting program in 1992, I enrolled in a Master of Business Administration.

The pressure of work, studies, and ill health all weighed on my physical and mental state; however, I was determined to continue with my regimented routine. Crunch time came when I fainted one day at home and Joe rushed to my aid.

I soon came to and tried to get up.

"Are you all right?" Joe asked.

I was in the course of replying when I collapsed again.

When I came around, I was able to visit the family doctor. I explained what had happened and complained about chest pains. The doctor sent me for chest X-rays, which showed an abnormally enlarged heart, and I was referred to a cardiologist.

The cardiologist undertook nuclear magnetic resonance imaging that involved injecting small amounts of radioactive material into my body to obtain images and information on my heart and heart function.

"It appears you have a build-up of fluid around

your heart, a condition referred to as pericardial effusion," the cardiologist advised, and he admitted me to hospital.

The casualty department quickly went to work, administering a couple of injections into my chest. "We've given you a local anaesthetic," the doctor explained. "However, if you feel any pain, let us know."

The doctor inserted a tube to drain the fluid and suggested the procedure could be viewed via the ultrasound. I watched the screen with intrigue as the tube made its way through my chest, precariously close to my beating heart.

My condition stabilised and I was advised that I could soon be transferred to a ward. I was exceptionally relieved when they removed the tube from my chest and my fever subsided.

My family visited and assembled around my hospital bed. There was Mary, Joe, Jessica, my brother-in-law, Beau, five-year-old nephew Milton, and two-year-old niece Rose.

I looked at them and reflected on what I was doing with my life. Work and studies had occupied so much of my time, I wondered whether I had neglected the most important thing in my life — my family.

The diagnosis was that the splenectomy performed after my traffic accident during my overseas trip had impaired my immune system, making me prone to illness. It was recommended that I take oral antibiotics for life.

My circumstances caused me to struggle during that semester's studies. I had completed my research papers prior to hospitalisation; however, I only had a couple of weeks before my exams and I was grossly underprepared. Nevertheless, I struggled on and managed to get through.

I maintained regular check-ups with my doctor over the ensuing years and he suggested I might wish to follow up with a specialist concerning my lifelong antibiotics. The specialist advised that there had been continual developments in medicine and that I may no longer need to take daily doses.

I was thoroughly examined and prescribed a series of one-off vaccinations, with single booster injections in a month and five years' time. I was also recommended to keep an emergency supply of antibiotics on hand and to have my name placed on a Spleen Register, to keep me abreast of any medical updates. I was content with the various vaccinations and boosters, as it relieved me of having to take antibiotic pills every single day for the rest of my life.

I felt that I had accomplished a great deal in the last four years and that it might be time for a change. It didn't come as a complete shock to my parents when I told them of my decision to leave home. The issue had been raised in conversation a number of times and it was now simply a matter of when.

The day of my departure came around, which I seemed to put off by the week and then by the day. I couldn't think of any more excuses to delay my leaving, though, and I prepared for my goodbyes. I took my remaining possessions and made my way to the lounge. My parents were both seated and one of the neighbours had popped in. "Oh well. I'm off now," I stated.

The neighbour was in the middle of explaining something, so I waited some time before trying again. "I'm leaving now."

The neighbour looked at me with an annoyed expression, as if I had unnecessarily interrupted her. "I'm leaving home now," I confirmed.

"Oh, goodbye Frank," the neighbour replied.

Mary and Joe each gave me a kiss and we said goodbye. The neighbour continued with her gossiping and I remained stationary for a moment before I made my exit.

It was a lonely drive to my property. After I entered the house, I walked in and out of every soulless room. I had an overwhelming hollow feeling and a wave of sorrow came over me. I had thoughts of returning to the family home, but I knew my sense of emptiness was something I had to endure.

# Chapter 29

# High Anxiety

The Audit Office in Melbourne continued in a state of flux. The contracting out of work to the private sector had now become an integral part of operations, particularly during peak periods.

Work that previously had been completed on a routine basis by Audit Office staff was now considered to be a major work pressure. This was the case whether it was to meet commercial deadlines on compliance or performance audits, or to table departmental and other annual reports in parliament as soon as possible.

The Audit Office executives stressed the need to supplement its staff's expertise by contracting the best available talent from external sources, which was promoted as a valuable two-way exchange of knowledge.

In reality, the Audit Office staff had much more practical and technical knowledge of the auditees, and the flow of information and knowledge only went one way. The external contractors and auditors were like sponges, as they were effectively provided with training that would place them in prime position for an eventual takeover.

Nevertheless, there was constant criticism of Audit Office staff and a push for the work to be handled by external auditors. The view was that the successful implementation of commercialisation, devolution of authority, and risk management required substantive change in the public sector culture.

As the pressure for change intensified, the messages from the Audit Office executive took a more serious tone. It was now openly being communicated that poor performers in auditing would not have other avenues for their productive employment and this would put at risk the job we were charged to perform for the government, parliament, and the taxpayer.

The message was offensive to Audit Office staff, many of whom held nothing higher than their public service to the community.

\*    \*    \*

Gentleman Jim and Ron continued to be my close friends in the office, and we maintained our socialising over coffee breaks, lunch, and after-work drinks on Fridays.

I considered it curious that both Jim and Ron seemed oblivious to my facial abnormalities, just as I had been oblivious to them during the years of my early childhood.

Gentleman Jim was slim and of average height,

while Ron was over six foot and burly; however, notwithstanding their differences in strength and stature, whenever I encountered any form of abuse, both of them would unhesitatingly back me up and support me.

One day, when I entered a bar with Jim and Ron, there was a bartender who we all recognised as a smart alec.

"Are you a boxer?" the bartender asked me, wearing a mischievous grin.

"No," I curtly replied. "Why do you ask?"

"Oh, nothing," the bartender said as he burst into laughter.

Jim and Ron didn't pick up on the insinuation made by the bartender, but I certainly did. The bartender was suggesting I looked like a boxer because my head appeared as if it had been repeatedly beaten up.

On another occasion, when we attended the same bar, Jim and Ron were more attuned to what was going on. The bar was full of people when I went to order a round of drinks.

"How's it going, Mickey?" the bartender asked me, wearing his customary grin.

I proceeded to place my order when Jim interrupted. "Why are you calling him Mickey?"

"Don't worry about it," I suggested, as I knew exactly what the bartender meant.

The bartender was still smiling. "Well, with those ears, he looks like Mickey Mouse."

The bartender laughed, as did a number of patrons who had overheard the comment.

Jim and Ron both reacted strongly, with Jim hurling abuse and Ron almost jumping the bar.

"Come on, guys." I intervened, taking hold of Ron. "Maybe we don't need to be drinking at this bar."

Jim patted me on the shoulder. "Yeah. Let's get out of this hell hole."

Jim and I made our way out, pulling Ron along, while he stared daggers at the bartender. We never went back to that bar.

# Chapter 30

## Facial Recognition

I was having trouble sleeping and I suspected it was due to the pressures at work. I regularly woke during the night, gasping for air. After discussing my issue with a few friends, I decided to get it checked out.

I briefed my doctor, who examined me before referring me to an Ear, Nose and Throat specialist. The specialist took little time in assessing my condition. "You have a severe deviated septum. In fact, it's so bad your right nostril is almost completely blocked. Close your left nostril and try to breathe through the right."

I did so, and I could hardly breathe at all.

"Have you ever had a heavy knock to your nose?" the specialist asked me.

"No."

"That's strange. I guess it's congenital."

*That's not strange at all,* I thought. *In fact, it's obvious that I've had a number of abnormalities from birth.*

The specialist continued. "The extent of deviation is so extreme that medication will not assist you. I would recommend a septoplasty." My confused look caused the specialist to further explain. "This involves corrective surgery to straighten the deviated nasal septum."

After a few days of reflection, I visited my parents and advised them of the prognosis. As usual, they gave me their unwavering support. During my visit, Jessica also made an appearance and I briefed her as well.

"Are you also going to have a nose job?" she asked in a blasé fashion.

"No. I hadn't even thought about that."

"I just thought that if you were going through all that trouble, why not have a nose job as well?"

"I suppose it couldn't hurt to ask," I replied, pensively.

During my follow-up appointment with the specialist, I raised the matter of a nose job.

"Of course I can perform a rhinoplasty as well," the specialist keenly answered. "Although I'm not a plastic surgeon, I've performed many of them."

The specialist then showed me a number of before and after photographs of his previous patients. After I perused his portfolio, I looked up at him and he gave me an optimistic smile.

"Okay," I said. "Since I'm going to undergo surgery in any case, why not?"

The operation was performed in hospital under general anaesthetic and the specialist visited me the following day. "How do you feel?" he asked.

"I feel okay."

"You should feel like you've been bashed around the head with a baseball bat, because that's basically what I did."

I struggled to laugh, but I could be heard emitting a slight chuckle.

After a couple of weeks, I returned to the specialist. "I think it looks good," he remarked. "It will look even better once all the swelling goes down and the excess skin in your nostrils contracts as the skin redrapes evenly with normal healing."

It took a couple of months for the healing process to take hold and it made a dramatic improvement to my breathing. I was satisfied with the result, especially since I did not notice any more name-calling concerning my nose. Although my other abnormal facial features attracted the usual, if not increased, attention.

After several months, I had trouble sleeping again, but now it wasn't caused by breathing problems; instead, it was from sore jaw joints and severe headaches. I persevered with the condition for a few weeks before I visited my doctor.

Again, my doctor referred me to a specialist, this time an orthodontist. The orthodontist examined my jaw and the inside of my mouth, over and over.

"You seem to have an extreme case of prognathism, being a protruding jaw, which in your case is a protruding lower jaw, or underbite," the orthodontist explained as he further pondered the matter. "It would not be effective to treat your current condition with braces alone. I suggest that you would also need to consider maxillofacial surgery."

The moment I heard this I was taken aback. I was well aware that I had a number of abnormal features, but I'd always expected they were cosmetic rather than structural. I was therefore intrigued with what a surgeon would have to say.

The surgeon routinely examined me and quickly gave his prognosis. "I have examined the referral and the X-rays provided by the orthodontist and I agree with his view. You have structural misalignment of your jaw, with a distinctive lower jaw protrusion, and this condition is exacerbated by your under-grown upper jaw. The only way your condition can be properly corrected is by surgery."

"It sounds fairly extreme," I said.

"It is extreme," the surgeon advised. "The process is quite extensive, whereby the orthodontic procedure would need to be coordinated with the surgery."

I was shocked. "So how long would all this take?"

"The initial orthodontic work usually takes a year or two. The surgery would be performed in hospital under general anaesthesia, which will require a stay of a few days and convalescing at home for a few weeks. During this time, you will be on a liquid diet, and I don't mean alcohol," the specialist said with a smile. "The post surgery orthodontic work also usually takes a year or two."

I quickly added up all the time components in my

head and tried to take in what I had heard before I uttered anything. "I'll have to think about this," I eventually said.

I returned to my doctor and sought another referral for a second opinion. As I expected, the prognosis and the recommended course of action from the specialists were the same.

I confided in a few friends and one of them recommended a doctor with a special interest in jaw conditions who practiced alternative forms of medicine and had apparently done wonders. *What the hell*, I thought. *I may as well give him a try*.

The doctor was highly optimistic. "Oh, I'm sure I'd be able to remedy your jaw pain and headaches," he boasted as he pulled out a contraption. "I have developed my own protective headgear you can wear at night that will stop the jaw movement that is causing you pain."

"So I wear this headgear at night while I sleep?"

"This is a prototype and I would need to custom make one to fit you, but it would be something like this."

"And for how long would I need to apply this headgear?"

"Well, all your life, of course."

I couldn't get out of the clinic fast enough. I considered up to four years of orthodontic procedure and surgery as an appealing prospect compared to having to wear ridiculous headgear in bed at night for the rest of my life.

The family supported my decision, even though the look of concern on their faces was obvious. However, my parents were heartened by the fact that I would need to move back to the family home for a few weeks over the period of my recovery from surgery.

I was immensely self-conscious about wearing braces, particularly at my advanced age of 32 years. If I was antisocial before the orthodontic procedure, I was now a virtual loner. Other than going to work, the only other place I visited was the family home a couple of times a week.

As the time for the surgery neared, the surgeon instructed me to undertake the necessary preparations. These included taking iron supplements and donating blood, so the hospital had it on standby during the surgery.

I was happy with my orthodontist and surgeon. Both of them explained every detail and addressed all my questions and concerns. I was also comforted by the fact that they were reputedly leaders in their respective fields.

I underwent the operation and my surgeon visited me the following day, greeting me with his usual bright smile.

"How are you feeling?"

"My jaw doesn't feel too bad," I struggled to say. "But my hip really hurts."

"That's where we removed some bone that we inserted into your upper jaw in order to support it," the surgeon explained. "It will be painful, that's normal, but you'll need to get mobilised by walking around as soon as possible ahead of your discharge."

Later in the day, I attempted to get up, but I found the pain in my hip too agonising. It felt like my skin and tissue were being torn apart.

A nurse entered. "Haven't you got up yet?"

"I tried, but the pain is excruciating."

"I understand that, but you need to start walking around as you are due to leave hospital in the next day or two."

"Don't you have any crutches?" I asked.

The nurse gave me a quizzical look. "I've never seen anyone use crutches; they just walk out. You need to force yourself."

I compelled myself to get up, although I continued complaining. "This really does hurt, you know."

The nurse gave me a wry smile.

After my discharge, I spent a couple of weeks with my parents at the family home. I was being spoiled all over again and I loved it. I was so comfortable I didn't want to leave, but I did.

I spent a further week convalescing at my house before I returned to work and rejoined the usual doom and gloom of the Audit Office environment.

My manager was the first to see me. "So how are you going?" asked Mr Meaney.

"I'm much better, thanks."

"You know, there are people who think the operations you are having are just cosmetic," he said.

I looked at him without uttering a word. I never thought to have any of my surgical procedures to make me look better, although I was hopeful that they would correct my abnormalities to stop the name-calling and bullying.

"They think you're vain," he added.

I gave him a wry smile, as I suspected the people he was referring to included himself. "People can think whatever they like," I said. "Even if they are ignorant of the facts or just plain ignorant."

Mr Meaney gave me a serious staring down and appeared to be deliberating over something for a while, until he released what was on his mind. "You know, I've been told that even when people have cosmetic surgery, it doesn't change a person's genes, so their offspring are still likely to inherit their parents' original features."

I returned his stare with some curiosity and was not at all offended by his remark. In fact, I had previously considered the view as being factual and didn't have a problem with it. Nevertheless, as I knew Mr Meaney's sentiments were mean-spirited, I felt obliged to respond.

"I don't feel that it's an issue for me, as I don't expect I'll ever have any children," I said. "But I guess every prospective parent would wish the best for their children, and everyone should wish that every child is born healthy and happy."

# Chapter 31

## One Door Closes

The patience of the senior executives in the Audit Office was wearing thin as, year after year, the government failed to act on the recommendations in the Report of the Committee of Public Accounts that had been tabled back in April 1989.

After four years, the Audit Office proceeded to take matters into its own hands and to wield a big stick to organise and operate the Audit Office in a way considered appropriate and in line with recommendations from the Report. The main objective was stated to be the need to compete with the private sector and to deliver a commercial, quality, and professional service.

The plan for the Audit Office from the 1993—1994 financial year was to put in place a new structure that supported a mix of Audit Office staff and private sector auditors, particularly where commercial and specialist skills were claimed to be required.

The private sector auditors were also seen as the answer to alleviate the problems caused by high workloads with short deadlines requiring a concentration of resources for short periods. On the other hand, permanent Audit Office employees were seen as obstacles in productively meeting workloads, as they caused overstaffing during the quieter periods.

The contracting out of auditing work was compounded by the level of privatisation of public entities. Australia followed the United Kingdom's lead with one of the largest programs of privatisation among OECD countries, with the value of privatisations in Australia during the 1990s ranking second after the United Kingdom and second relative to Gross Domestic Product after New Zealand.

Whilst the Audit Office had been engaging external accounting firms for some years, it was now proposing to engage them in earnest. At the same time, a voluntary redundancy program commenced from the 1992—1993 financial year.

The Audit Office also introduced performance-based pay to reward the contribution of senior officers in achieving the office's goals and to motivate staff. However, in reality, the financial rewards went only to senior officers who essentially met the goals due to the hard work and dedication of the lower level, operative staff, who received nothing. Instead of motivating staff, the initiative further lowered staff morale.

In response to the various changes in the Audit Office, the Union served a log of claims that was the subject of ongoing negotiations with Industrial Relations.

The writing was now well and truly on the wall and the Audit Office staff in Melbourne prepared for the worst. Their careers were now in danger, as they were looking to become an extinct species.

*     *     *

Feeling down, I arranged a catch-up with Heston to get the depression of my work situation off my chest. However, just like our previous conversation, since both our jobs had many common areas of concern, our discussion did little to appease our dispirited moods.

The Audit Office and the Tax Office were both impacted by the public service reform agenda, which required eking out efficiency dividends through job losses while bringing in external consultants or contracting out work at a higher cost. Both organisations had promotion and appeal systems that promulgated a meritorious process when it actually just went through the motions and ended up promoting their preordained favourites. Both organisations had performance systems that rewarded senior officers who did little to achieve targets, while the actual workers missed out, resulting in lower staff motivation and morale.

Heston appeared as miserable as I felt, although he seemed to perk up when I explained the additional problems overpowering the Audit Office as a result of redefining the audit mandate to expand functions from financial statement audits to performance audits, all while transferring the work from the public to the private sector.

"The situation in the Audit Office seems utterly insane," Heston commented. "Since the Tax Office commenced the Large Case Audit Program on the top 100 companies, we've seen firsthand the shoddy work conducted by the private sector audits. What can one really expect when there are obvious conflicts of interest, with the companies paying the private entity firms enormous fees? In my view, rather than the Audit Office contracting out the auditing work of public sector organisations to the private sector, the public sector should be undertaking all audit compliance work, both on the public-sector organisations as well as on private-sector firms. What the Audit Office is doing is the equivalent of the Tax Office contracting out taxation audits or Defence contracting out going to war to the private sector. It's pure madness!"

"I actually hadn't looked at it in those terms. I've been more concerned about the distinct prospect of losing my job," I replied. "But I see the rationale in your argument."

"The executive in the Tax Office often reply to our grievances by stating we're lucky to have a job. I now appreciate what they mean, as you guys appear to be screwed," Heston said. "Thanks, Frank. You've made me feel a lot better about my career, but good luck with yours. It sounds like you're really going to need it."

# Chapter 32

## Plastic Surgery

I had resolved that my future career belonged outside the Audit Office. I was fortunate to have been assigned audits where I got on well with the managers of the entities, and where I worked alongside external auditors. My diligent approach and my natural enthusiasm towards my work seemed to have made a good impression, as it resulted in a couple of invitations to apply for a job.

The prospect of a change in career and, in effect, the closing of a chapter in my life, made me consider fixing my remaining facial abnormality: my asymmetrical, protruding ears.

I laboured the idea for some time before I caught up with Heston at a pub. We were leaning against the bar, engaged in conversation, when an inebriated man bumped into me. The moment he laid eyes on me, he uttered, "It's the Elephant Man."

Instantaneously, my mind in respect of having an ear operation was made up.

My doctor referred me to an otoplasty surgeon in the outer eastern suburbs of Melbourne. After the initial consultation, the surgeon made arrangements for a procedure to be performed under local anaesthetic at his private clinic.

I had a strange feeling as I drove to the clinic. I was nervous, as if I had butterflies in my stomach. Nevertheless, I was convinced that what I was doing was the right thing for me.

The surgeon made me feel at ease and administered local anaesthetic injections around my ears. He checked with me that my ears and the surrounding areas were numb before he commenced the surgery.

I could feel cutting, pulling, and tugging sensations as calm enveloped me. I reacted with a slight smile, and then, for no reason I could decipher, a tear developed in my left eye and slowly trickled down my cheek.

The surgeon provided a running commentary as he conducted the procedure, mentioning the intricacies required due to the differing forms between my two ears. The challenging nature of the operation resulted in a longer-than-usual duration.

"Do you feel any pain?" the surgeon asked me at the end of the surgery.

"I feel okay."

"The procedure has taken longer than the standard operation,' the surgeon said. "I can give you some analgesic pills."

"I should be all right," I replied.

I left the clinic feeling uncomfortable, mainly due to the head bandages. I was driving home when I started to feel discomfort behind my ears. I had made it roughly halfway before the pain became intense. I still had about twenty minutes to go, and it was now excruciating. *It can't get much worse than this*, I thought, but it then increased another few notches.

I was moaning and groaning by the time I arrived home. I parked the car, rushed inside, and raided the paracetamol. I then collapsed on the couch and reflected: *No pain, no gain.*

# Chapter 33

## Another Door Opens

The Melbourne staff's greatest fears were realised when, as part of the voluntary redundancy program, their numbers were decimated.

The Audit Office staff in the Melbourne regional office reduced from 110 in 1992, to 85 in 1993, 47 in 1994, 32 in 1995, 31 in 1996, 21 in 1997, and 18 in 1998. The office was officially closed on Wednesday, 31 March 1999.

The regional offices in Brisbane, Adelaide, and Perth had already closed, and the representative presence in London had also ceased. Nationally, the overall staff levels in the Audit Office reduced from 637 in 1992 to 284 in 1999.

As the dust settled, some Audit Office staff in Melbourne came out the other end in a good position, while others did not do so well. Most auditors were redeployed in other government departments. A number were hired by government business enterprises and privatised government corporations. Several took a redundancy package and retired early, yet a few obtained a redundancy package but could not find ongoing, regular employment.

Jim was almost 55 and was ecstatic to receive a golden handshake as well as being able to take advantage of the old superannuation scheme, which would allow him to resign and go onto a lucrative superannuation pension.

Ron was relieved to have found redeployment in another government department in Melbourne, as an internal auditor, where, unlike in many other redeployments, he could effectively make use of his extensive, long-gained auditing knowledge.

I was crossing my fingers as I had two job interviews, one with a government business enterprise and the other with a government privatised corporation.

I was desperate to escape the Audit Office, as my only other option was to accept a government redeployment. I was not at all enthused about this prospect as I was desperate to leave the environment of the public sector. Even though I considered the public service to be a noble occupation, management treated its staff like office fodder. Furthermore, by remaining as a government employee, I would not be entitled to a golden handshake.

I attended the two interviews and I thought both went well. I was heartened that the interviewers in both cases seemed to place a high value on my postgraduate studies and professional accreditations, which was in stark contrast to the ridicule and criticisms I received in the Audit Office.

I was over the moon when both firms offered me

a job, and I deliberated for some days, trying to figure out which one I should accept. In the end, I grabbed a coin and made the Enterprise heads and the Corporation tails. I flipped the coin. It came up tails.

At one stage, the Audit Office benchmarked the various ASO positions against external market positions and my new position as Internal Auditor in the Corporation had been benchmarked as equivalent to an ASO 6 position; however, my pay was going to be markedly better.

Furthermore, I was one of the last staff to leave the Audit Office in Melbourne, which allowed me to tick over 17 years of seniority. The significance of this was that I would be eligible for a greater benefit under the voluntary redundancy package.

The standard voluntary redundancy package was two weeks' pay for every year of service up to a maximum of 48 weeks, plus an additional four weeks' pay. Therefore, I should have been entitled to 34 weeks plus 4 weeks' pay, amounting to a total of 38 weeks. However, due to the vagaries of the voluntary redundancy offers, as I had completed over 17 years of service, I would be granted the full 48 weeks plus the additional 4 weeks, being 52 weeks, effectively amounting to a full year's salary. The cherry on top was that the full amount was tax free.

If things were not already good enough, I would also be paid out all my unused annual leave and long service leave. Any accumulated sick leave would have been lost; however, as I had used most of my sick

237

leave on my illnesses and surgical procedures, I hardly had any left.

The upshot was that I would be eligible for a huge, tax-free golden handshake and moving on to a better job with a greater salary. It was a possible win, win, win!

These fortunate events made it seem as though all my stars were aligning and this period of my life was turning out to be a truly eureka moment.

Contrary to my situation, Mr Meaney planned to stay in the Audit Office, but as they were closing the regional office in Melbourne, his only hope was to go to Canberra; however, as the overall staff numbers were being rationalised, there was little chance of that. He was 50 years old, which was too young to retire, and he was unlikely to find a comparable job outside the public service. He wasn't taking the situation well and was making life difficult for everyone else.

I made a point of not telling Mr Meaney that I had gained a job with the Corporation. He didn't like me and I was sure the news of my good fortune would further infuriate him.

I was the last person to leave the Melbourne regional office. On my last day of work, I had the responsibility of switching off the lights. I felt it was symbolic, as it was also lights-out on my Audit Office career.

In 1999, at the age of 38, I commenced a completely new phase of my life with a different job and a fresh facial appearance.

*   *   *

I hit the ground running with the Corporation. I was enormously grateful for the opportunity, I was eager to learn, and felt blessed with the chance to start my career anew.

I was lucky to have been on the Audit Office section assigned the external audit of the Corporation, where I conducted compliance and performance audits. The experience provided me with an in-depth knowledge of their corporate structure, their financial accounts, and their overall operations. Without this experience, I would have had a steep learning curve and it would have been a challenge to build the necessary networks and connections.

I found the work varied and, at times, demanding, but I relished the environment where I had good working relationships with the audit staff, the finance personnel, and the executive. I was very much looking forward to my new career.

# Chapter 34

## One Night Stands

Since Heston got married and my Audit Office friends moved on, the Friday after-work drink sessions became less frequent. I commenced my new job and found myself mixing with a broader, eclectic social group from the Corporation and affiliated companies, as well as their associates and friends. I also attended more fashionable and popular bars and clubs.

I had tremendous difficulty fitting into the social environment, where I found myself circling the room and engaging in trivial chit-chat with acquaintances. However, after a sufficient number of libations, I felt a little more comfortable and was drawn into conversations with the ladies.

I was particularly conscious of the various cliques and how certain women generally seemed to be attracted to particular types of men. It appeared that the more stunning females were drawn to men with good looks, wealth, and/or entertainment value, but I didn't fit into any of these categories.

Nevertheless, I did notice distinct differences since my facial reconstruction. Whereas previously I was avoided and received no attention from the women, I now had some approaches and was encountering more normal reactions.

To my surprise, sometimes even reasonably attractive women talked to me. I was complimented by this and was flattered when they exhibited delightful personalities and engaged in interesting conversation.

One woman I met was a popular socialite named Katie. She was a budding artistic painter who had etched a successful career as a freelance interior decorator. I enjoyed her company until the night drew to a close, at which point I was about to bid her goodbye.

"You're not going, are you?" she asked me.

"I'd invite you home, but I don't think you'd be able to keep up with me to catch the last train to Upfield," I joked.

Katie smiled. "Well, you could always come back to my place."

I was flabbergasted. I wasn't sure whether she was just joking and I didn't know what to say. I was then struck by her dazzling pearly whites as she smiled at me, and her fluttering eyelids seemed to suggest she was sincere, in which case, I couldn't say no.

Katie drove us to her apartment in the inner eastern suburbs. Even though I felt a little out of place, she made me comfortable. "*Mia casa, sua casa,*" she said.

Katie offered me a beer and then asked, "Do you

want a joint?"

I had never indulged in the substance and I looked into her eyes, filled with anticipation, and automatically replied. "Why not?"

Katie skilfully rolled a cigarette with a mixture of tobacco and marijuana. She sucked on it as she lit it and then passed it to me. I took a few drags and handed it back as she led me onto her back veranda. We alternated the smoke as we sipped our drinks.

After we had finished the cigarette and our drinks, I was about to bid her goodbye again when she made another offer. "Would you like to spend the night?"

I was dumbstruck, although I tried to disguise my surprise. "Sure. Why not?" I confidently replied.

I was uncertain of her actual intentions, so I just followed her lead. She walked out the room and I trailed her into her bedroom. She then started to take off her clothes.

I stood there admiring her. She had a shapely figure, with pale-white skin. She got down to her underwear and jumped into bed.

I undressed down to my underpants and joined her. The moment I got into bed, she spoke abruptly. "By the way, I don't have sex on the first date."

I was still, like a statue. Her statement should have disappointed me; however, I actually felt relieved. "That's okay," I said as I cuddled up against her, and we fell asleep in each other's arms.

I was up at around 10.00 a.m. with a splitting headache and started to get dressed.

"Would you like some breakfast?" Katie asked.

"No thanks. I'd better be going," I replied. "Could you call me a cab?"

We kissed when the taxi arrived and I left. During the ride I was feeling queasy and I asked the driver to pull over. As he parked by the side of the road, I got out and puked in the gutter. After composing myself, I got back into the cab.

"Are you going to be all right?" the cabbie asked.

"I should be okay," I answered.

The following Friday, I joined the same acquaintances at the same bar. Lo and behold, I saw Katie and she was quick to approach me. We had a fun conversation and she monopolised my time for the rest of the night. It was almost natural for me to ask her back to my place and she automatically accepted.

We caught a taxi to my house and I offered her a drink and a cigarette. We sat on the couch, chatting, drinking, and smoking. As the night drew on, I felt as if it was preordained that I should invite her to spend the night. She accepted.

I escorted Katie to my bedroom and she undressed, but this time she stripped naked before she jumped into bed. Again, I followed her lead.

As soon as I made myself comfortable next to her, she spoke. "You do know that I'm not having sex?"

I wasn't bothered either way, but I thought I'd be playful. "Why not?"

"Why would you think I would want to have sex?"

"Well, last time you mentioned that you didn't have sex on the first date, but this is our second encounter, so I guessed you would want to have sex."

Katie didn't reply. Instead, she turned away from me and planted her cool buttocks against my groin. I settled down and got comfortable, while she nestled her backside into me and started swaying it from side to side. I was starting to get excited and developed a strong erection.

Katie did not let up and I was getting so horny I started to rub up to her, thrusting my penis against her until I ejaculated all over her arse cheek. She reacted by getting up, slapping me on the shoulder, and heading to the bathroom wearing a cheeky grin.

I stayed in bed feeling enormously ashamed. Katie returned, and I took my turn in the bathroom to wash up. When I returned, I got back into bed and we cuddled up and fell asleep.

In the morning, we got up at the same time and had some breakfast. I drove her home and gave her a kiss as I dropped her off. We didn't say much that morning and we didn't get in touch with each other during the week.

The next Friday, I had a choice of going to the bar where I had met Katie or going to another bar. I elected to go to the other bar. I subsequently heard, through word of mouth, that Katie also didn't go back to that bar, and I never saw nor heard from her again.

*    *    *

I had developed flexible social habits with a number of work colleagues and friends, as well as transitory socialites whom I bumped into at various bars and clubs.

I was happily drunk as I mingled with a group at a bar when I was introduced to three young women. My first impressions were that two of them were pretty and the third was gorgeous. I soon learned that the gorgeous woman had a boyfriend, which made me think, *That'd be right.*

I was left chatting with the other two until I excused myself to go to the toilet. Upon my return, I noted that only one of the women remained.

"Thanks for hanging around to mind my drink," I said.

"It was my pleasure, Frank."

"Sorry, what was your name again?"

"It's Grace."

I noticed that Grace had finished her drink. "Would you like another?"

"No, that's all right. I was going to leave soon."

There was a period of silence as I finished my beer.

"I recall you mentioning that you live in Carlton," Grace said. "It's on my way home, so I'd be happy to give you a lift."

I didn't really think too much about the offer before I answered, "Sure. Why not?"

Grace drove me home and I automatically asked whether she'd like to come in. I asked out of courtesy, rather than anything else, so it was a surprise to me when she accepted.

I was sloshed and very tired as I shuffled inside and guided Grace into the living room, taking a seat on the couch.

"Would you like a drink or something?"

"No, I'm fine, thanks."

I had no idea what to say or do, as all I desired was to get to sleep. Grace just sat there, smiling. I felt we had exhausted all the popular speaking topics at the bar, and I really didn't want to force a conversation.

"I'm feeling pretty zonked, so I might hit the sack," I said. Grace remained seated, not saying a word, and continued smiling. I was at a total loss as to what to say. "Did you want to stay the night?" I eventually blurted out.

"Oh, okay."

I led Grace to my bedroom, wondering what the hell I was doing. I dressed down to my underpants and jumped into bed. Grace undressed completely and joined me.

"Goodnight," I was quick to say as I rolled over, facing away from her.

"Goodnight," she replied.

In the morning, I woke on the edge of the bed, with Grace hard up against me. I turned over, which caused her to give up some space. We were facing each other, although she had her eyes closed, and she began to cuddle up next to me. I then started to feel penile stimulation and soon developed a hard-on. I tried to pull my groin away from her, but she had already felt my erection and she rammed her hips into me.

Grace got hold of my cock and milked me like a cow. I didn't resist and we kissed passionately. She took little time to mount me, bouncing up and down while she grunted and moaned. I remained lying down, trying to keep pace with her.

I was starting to get tired and I sensed that she was too when, all of a sudden, she let out a loud shriek and began shaking.

"Are you all right?" I asked.

"Yeah, I'm fine," she responded, casually. "I just had an orgasm."

I didn't really think too much about it, other than being happy for her.

We stayed in bed for a little while before I got up and went to the bathroom. I was having a shower when Grace joined me. She kissed me passionately again, grabbing my penis, and giving me a hand job.

"Okay, that's enough," I said with a wry smile.

Grace was on her way home when she expressed her wish to see me again. I promised to give her a call.

Over the subsequent few days, I reflected on my experience with Grace. I didn't find her overly attractive, either physically or platonically, but I had never previously engaged in that form of primitive, uncivilised, bestial sex, and the thought excited me.

I rang Grace and agreed to have dinner on Saturday night at her place. I drove the short distance to her house in Thornbury and she warmly greeted me, allowing me to enter as I handed her a bottle of red wine.

As soon as I stepped inside, I smelled a strange odour. "What's cooking?" I asked.

"Steak and vegetables," she replied.

I was sure the odour did not emanate from a dead animal, as I thought it smelled a lot worse. When we made our way into the living room, the mystery was solved: there were several cats sleeping or lounging about.

"I guess this is the family," I quipped.

"I treat them as my family," she said.

We sat down to dinner, but I couldn't stop being distracted by her pets. Although they didn't seem to disrupt the mood of the evening, as the cats were the only topic of conversation.

After dinner, we lazed on the lounge suite, sipping red wine. We started kissing, but I couldn't get in the mood as the cats were all around us and they were really bothering me. It was only 9.30 p.m. when I had had enough.

"Well, I'd better be going," I said.

"Don't you want to stay the night?"

"It would be nice; however, I need to get up early tomorrow," I said, which was a lie, but I didn't feel in the least bit guilty about saying it, as my true feelings would have revealed negative thoughts and I didn't want to hurt her feelings.

I never saw nor heard from Grace again.

*     *     *

I continued to patronize various bars and clubs, getting drunk and socialising with a mix of friends and acquaintances. I sometimes enjoyed the events, but I eventually figured out that it was the drinking I enjoyed more than the people I met.

It took almost a year before I realised my lifestyle and the people I was socialising with were artificial, shallow, and hollow. I then wondered what I could do to improve my social life.

# Chapter 35

## The Dating Scene

During my time with the Corporation, I worked long hours and regularly brought work home during the week. I didn't mind this in the least as it forced me to develop a regimented routine that, counter-intuitively, resulted in my carving out more spare time.

After a couple of years in the new job, I reflected on my situation and sensed a void in my life. I thought I knew what it was: a woman who could be my companion, my girlfriend, my soul mate.

I registered with a dating agency as well as signing up with an internet dating site. I attended an interview with the dating agency, where a delightful, middle-aged woman greeted me and asked me a series of questions concerning my statistical and personal information.

She continually looked at me as she took down notes, as if she could decipher as much information from my body language and facial expressions as she could from my verbal responses.

She seemed to be genuinely surprised when I informed her that, at 40, I had never been in a relationship. Finally, she handed me a brochure that included their costs, which caused me to raise my eyebrows.

"Would you like to commit to one of our plans?" she asked.

"I'll have to give the matter some further thought," I replied.

I examined the brochure more closely when I arrived home. The least expensive plan was for one date a month for 10 months at a cost of $2,500.

The dating agency followed up the interview with a telephone call, but I declined all the plans.

"We can leave your name on our database," the female receptionist suggested. "We have many more females than males, so we might be in a position to offer you some complimentary bookings from time to time."

Over the ensuing months, I was offered several complimentary meetings with professional young women. They were doctors, lawyers, scientists, and women who were completing PhDs on the most obscure topics; however, for varying reasons, none of the meetings amounted to anything.

During the same time, I was also active on the internet dating site where I managed to arrange a number of meetings, but none of these amounted to anything either. I was about to take a break from the dating scene when I agreed to meet one more woman. That woman happened to be Dorothy.

# Chapter 36

# A Brief Relationship Ends

It was unexpected when Dorothy contacted me a week after our date and invited me for drinks in the city on Friday after work.

I had a tough week at the Corporation, where I had to meet tight reporting deadlines. I worked like a Trojan on the Friday to complete my tasks, but still arrived 20 minutes late.

I entered the popular city bar and had some trouble locating Dorothy. When I eventually tracked her down, I was surprised to find she had invited Prue, her closest friend. It was the first time I had met Prue, although Dorothy had previously mentioned her ad nauseam.

I purchased a round of drinks and tried to engage Prue in conversation. She seemed evasive, preferring to use Dorothy as her intermediary and mouthpiece.

I observed the two ladies whispering to each other at regular intervals and they often glanced over at me.

"We're leaving now," Dorothy soon announced.

"What?" I queried. "We're leaving now?"

"No, not you," she clarified. "Prue and I are leaving."

"Are you sure?" I asked, recognising the broader significance of the statement, being the finality of our association.

"Yes," Dorothy confirmed. "Prue and I are leaving."

I observed Prue lead Dorothy out of the bar, while I stayed on to finish my drink. I felt most upset with the course of events, although the more I thought about it, the more I entertained the thought that maybe Prue had done me a gigantic favour.

Even though I enjoyed Dorothy's company, it was obvious, at the age of 33, that her biological clock was ticking and her priority was to find a suitable partner for a serious, long-term relationship. It was also obvious that that partner was not me.

I polished off my drink and walked out onto the street. I took a deep breath and the fresh night air filled my lungs. As I strolled down the street, a smile emerged on my face and I experienced a tremendous feeling of liberation and freedom.

I didn't know whether I would ever find my soul mate, but I considered that it wasn't important for me to know. I had a feeling my life should be carefree and serendipitous. I was now comfortable in my skin and happy in my outlook. I would always wish for a partner to enhance my life, but if I didn't find one, then so be it. If I did manage to find one, that would be a bonus. I felt it was all in the lap of the gods.

# Epilogue

It had been a few years since I underwent my surgical procedures and I had no further health problems, nor had I been subjected to any abuse or name-calling. I therefore felt vindicated in my decisions to go ahead with them.

Having my mind freed from the fear or actuality of being ridiculed, I became more aware of my own tendencies and idiosyncrasies.

My peculiarities included automatically crossing the road to avoid crowds and veering away from people who were walking towards or around me. I also picked up on the fact that I robotically only left the house to go to the shops and other retail outlets during non-peak periods, not because it would take less time, but solely to avoid people.

I realised my oddities had evolved over many years from the bullying and abuse. I had developed a high level of sensitivity where I felt I could gauge the true nature and character of people by looking through their pretences to see who they really were, and I often didn't like what I saw. Therefore, instead of having to come into contact with people and deal with them, I tried everything to avoid them.

My life experiences had anecdotally proven to me

over and over again that everyone had a good side and a bad side. What brought out the best and worst in people seemed to depend on a number of contributing factors, such as their nurturing and upbringing during childhood, their teaching and guidance at school, and the accepted standards and culture of the community.

Over the years, I had experienced firsthand the worst side of people that could manifest itself in degenerate, primitive, and barbaric behaviour. I often asked myself how could such behaviour be tolerated, much less occur, in a so-called 'civilised society'?

On the other hand, I felt fortunate that I had been blessed during the course of my life, especially over my darkest hours, with exceptional people I could rely on and who provided me with a pivotal level of support.

There were friends during my formative years who had included me in social events and made me feel like an equal, such as Lou and Michael. There was a person who was not just a good friend, but who treated me more like family: Heston. There were people who had watched my back when my own defences were weak, namely Jim and Ron. There were people who had provided me opportunities when all opportunity seemed lost, like Mr Fairley. Most of all, there was my family, who gave me unwavering and enduring support, care, and love, even being prepared to sacrifice their lives for me.

Yes, there were special people in the world,

although I believed that they were rare. Even so, there might still be a special woman out there for me to share my life with. Who knows?

It then dawned on me that, notwithstanding the surgical procedures to correct my facial abnormalities that put a stop to the bullying, inside I was still the same scared little boy. Even though I had fixed my outward appearance, I still had an enormous way to go to heal my internal wounds.

*Should I now turn my mind to focusing on opening myself up to people and allowing them into my life?* I wondered, although I knew this would be easier said than done.

I recognised that I had a lot of self-development and soul-searching to do before I could productively move on with my life. I didn't know what fate had in store for me, but I did know, now I was comfortable in my own skin, I had the confidence in myself to face the future full on.

www.ingramcontent.com/pod-product-compliance
Lightning Source LLC
Chambersburg PA
CBHW070438120726
47910CB00003B/841